D1799324

DISTAFF

A SCIENCE FICTION ANTHOLOGY

BY FEMALE AUTHORS

Distaff

No part of this book may be reproduced or transmitted in any form without the proper written consent of the appropriate copyright holders listed below.

The stories in this book are fiction. Any resemblance to any person, living or dead, is purely coincidental.

All Rights Reserved.

"The Broken Man" by Jane O'Reilly. **Copyright** © 2019 Jane O'Reilly. Used by permission of the author.

"Space Rocks" by Kerry Buchanan. **Copyright** © 2019 Kerry Buchanan. Used by permission of the author.

"The Ice Man" by Rosie Oliver. **Copyright** © 2019 Rosie Oliver. Used by permission of the author.

"Holo-Sweet" by E. J. Tett. **Copyright** © 2019 E. J. Tett. Used by permission of the author.

"A Cold Night in H3-II" by Juliana Spink Mills. **Copyright** © 2019 Juliana Spink Mills. Used by permission of the author.

"The Colour of Silence" by Damaris Browne. **Copyright** © 2019 Damaris Browne. Used by permission of the author.

"My Little Mecha" by Shellie Horst. **Copyright** © 2019 Shellie Horst. Used by permission of the author.

"Ab Initio" by Susan Boulton. **Copyright** © 2019 Susan Boulton. Used by permission of the author.

"The Shadows are Us and They are the Shadows" by Jo Zebedee. **Copyright** © 2019 Jo Zebedee. Used by permission of the author.

Cover Art by Shellie Horst. **Copyright** © 2019 Shellie Horst. Used by permission of the artist.

Elements of the Distaff cover were created from stock images used in accordance with Creative Commons Licence CC0.

ISBN: 1074955007
ISBN-13: 978-1074955007

FOREWORD

Two chance comments on SFFChronicles led to the creation of ***Distaff*** – were there any science fiction anthologies written solely by women, and how many members of the forum were women writing science fiction?

The answer to the first was very few, and most included reprints rather than all original work, or a mix of science fiction and fantasy. As for the second, we had more than enough talented women who jumped at the chance to write a short story in their favourite genre, including some who'd already contributed to a best-selling SF anthology. Several of us are published authors, two are Amazon best-sellers and another achieved success in the Rainbow Awards.

We also boast a professional copy writer, a cover designer, and in Rosie Oliver a BSFA shortlisted editor, together with willing hands to help with everything from critiquing and setting up websites, to legal issues and publicity. Which means ***Distaff*** wasn't simply conceived and written by women, but has been edited, managed and produced by us and our women friends on SFFChronicles, together with support at all levels from fellow Chronners.

So here we are. All new work, all science fiction, and all by women -- putting SF into the distaff role.

We hope you enjoy the tales we've spun.

DISTAFF

CONTENTS

DISTAFF

ACKNOWLEDGMENTS

Thanks go to so many people that have made this co-operative science fiction anthology truly a joint venture, that it is not possible to list them all. Thank you, everyone, you know who you are.

Special thanks go to:

Brian G Turner for hosting the sffchronicles.com forum that allowed us to work together despite being scattered around the globe.

Shellie Horst for doing such a wonderful cover and promotional artwork.

Jo Zebedee for doing all the publicity and arranging book launches.

Juliana Spink Mills for promoting Distaff and managing the Distaff anthology website distaffanthology.wordpress.com.

Damaris Browne for her legal drafting skills.

Samanda Primeau and Rosie Oliver for editing Distaff.

DISTAFF

THE BROKEN MAN

Jane O'Reilly

Once, Earth had consisted entirely of seas and land. There was water, and there was rock. It was a simple and clean place, although not necessarily a peaceful one, for the seas raged and the rock split and cracked and tumbled. But their destruction was never more than the Earth could handle.

Then there were people.

People soon decided that they could do better than water and rock. They put their brightest and best minds together, and between them, they invented plastic. It was a miracle substance. It came in every colour and could be made into any shape that the imagination could devise, and it lasted forever.

The problem was that although people liked the idea of things that lasted forever, they didn't really want them in reality. Sometimes, they barely wanted them to last for the scant few seconds it took to pull a chocolate bar from a wrapper, or the few minutes that it took to carry their new dress from the shop to the car. When that time was up they threw the plastic things away because there is no value in something that is easily replaced.

But all that plastic had to go somewhere.

It went deep under the soil and into the rivers and the oceans. It blew at the sides of roads and tangled itself into the bushes and the trees. It accumulated in huge mountains, piling up in stinking heaps that grew and grew, but as long as people couldn't see them, they could pretend that those things weren't there, and they were quite happy with that.

Eventually, however, the people could no longer ignore the plastic. It strangled the trees and it choked the rivers and it spread into the places where people wanted to go, like the beach and the park and their pretty front garden. But by the time people realised what they had done, it was too late. They could not clean up their mess. They did not want to live with it, either, so they went up into the skies, which were clean and empty, and they built themselves homes amongst the clouds and once again forgot about the plastic.

But Earth did not forget.

The plastic gathered together in huge floating islands on the sea. Every day more bottles and lids and fishing nets and pipes and tubes and syringes came to those islands. They grew at an astonishing pace. And slowly, the creatures in the sea, which had been deformed and reformed by endless tiny flakes of colourful glitter and old chewing gum and microbeads, crawled out of the water and onto those islands, their bodies mutating as flesh and plastic combined. It went into their brains and they began to change in ways that no-one could have predicted. Still, they did what living things have always done. They adapted, they survived, and they reproduced, their children born into a world that was filthy and disgusting, a place they called home because they had never known any different.

Kiko was one of a thousand children born to parents who had left her long before she could hatch. As she had grown, her body had changed, the plastic that ran through her flesh slowly emitting the chemicals needed to produce limbs and lungs as well as tentacles and fins. Her flesh firmed just enough to hold shape out of water. Fins became elegant hands. She still glowed, but only when the conditions were right.

On this particular morning, which was just like any other, she swung her legs over the edge of her bunk and lowered herself to the floor. She pulled on thick socks and her boiler suit, which she'd found over in section four underneath a cracked toilet bowl and a bundle of random wires. The boiler suit was an unfortunate shade of yellow, but it covered her arms and legs and kept off the sun and that was more important.

She rubbed her translucent skin with the clean corner of an otherwise dirty cloth and ate a banana from her fruit basket. It was overripe and smelly, but it was a banana, and she came by them too infrequently to think of it as anything other than a marvel. The sweetness went up her nose holes. She enjoyed it very much.

Then she opened the door of her workshop and stepped out into the stink. The rubbish that had rained down overnight had cluttered her path so she was forced to kick her way through. Fortunately her boots were solid enough to let nothing in, so she kicked with enthusiasm. This was her favourite time. You never knew what might have fallen quite literally into your path overnight. Usually it was nothing but junk, but sometimes, just sometimes, there might be something more.

Something glinted up ahead now and she pounced on it, dropping into a crouch and sweeping aside scattered pieces of snapped crockery and broken glass and rusted metal.

It was something most unexpected. A beautiful velvet glove. The fingers were long and elegant, the cuff exquisitely embroidered with green leaves and orange flowers. She glanced quickly around before she grabbed it. It slid free with no effort at all, and revealed something that set Kiko's heart truly to racing. No. No, it could not be! It should not be! Dropping the glove, she dug more, tossing aside bits and pieces of nothing until she came to a large panel with a crack like a bolt of lightning in the centre. She pushed it aside.

There, underneath it, was a man. Kiko looked him over once, then again, just to make sure that she had the detail of him. She looked around. None of the other pickers were up yet. And then, finally, she looked up at the cloud city. He could not have come from anywhere else. He most certainly had not come from here. His skin was too soft; there were no gill slits on his neck. His hair wasn't slimy and there were no whiskers trailing from his cheeks, or shells anywhere. His skin didn't look like the skin of the creatures that lived on the island. It shone with health and vitality. There were no sores, no flaking patches.

There were stripes down the sides of his midnight blue trousers, and his boots were shiny and at his hip was a sword, and she wondered at the games that were played in the cities in the sky that would require a man to be dressed in such a fashion.

She rolled him over. He was very heavy.

She had seen men before, at the market. But she was not sure she had ever seen one as well made as this. Who would throw him away? He was broken, of course, terribly broken, but there was still such great beauty in his face and the shape of his arms and legs. She crouched down beside him and gave him a prod. He made no sound, but she could see he was still breathing in his feeble human way. He was, somehow, alive.

If she left him here, Riak might take him, because he had a licence for this sort of thing, whereas Kiko was limited to carrier bags and other low-grade rubbish. She hoped to upgrade her licence in a year or so, but at the moment she was stuck until she had reached her quota.

Her fingers again closed round the beautiful glove. It was so soft, the colours fresh and glorious. She wouldn't take it, she decided. She just wanted to touch it. Reluctantly, she forced herself finally to leave it where it was. But she picked close to the man, close enough to watch and see what he did, which turned out to be nothing.

She filled her bag with flattened shampoo bottles and broken water tubes, not even bothering to check if they were clean. It wasn't until soap slimed her fingers that she stopped to look down at her hands and cursed herself for a fool for picking up a half empty one.

The bottle slithered from her grasp and bounced across the ground. She did not bother to chase it down. She should not have picked it up in the first place. This was not a good day to pick. The level of toxic gases emitted by the rubbish was rising more quickly than usual. The warning badge on her boiler suit was already at amber, and the ravenous stars, which crawled out from their hiding places when the sun was high, were already starting to appear.

But the man was still there. There was no sign of Riak, and the sun was getting high. If she left the man, he would die.

Dammit.

She could not leave him where he was, not when he could be repaired.

Kiko walked up to the man and grabbed his arm and pulled on it. He only slid a little way along the path, so she dug her heels in and heaved on his weight. She dragged him to her workshop, kicked the mechanism that would start the door rolling up, and then dragged him inside.

The door dropped down just in time to slice a star in half. It stared up at her with a hundred dead black eyes. She gave it the finger in return, and felt quite justified in doing so, for its brothers had chewed through her cables and half of her food supply the previous week, and to say she was not fond of them would be something of an understatement. Not everything that came out of the sea had evolved as she had. Some things had remained basic. Some things were just mean.

She rolled up the door just enough to kick the half star back outside, dropping it again before anything else could get in. Then she pushed a trolley over to where the man lay. She managed to get him onto it using a combination of pushing, pulling, and swearing, then jacked it up to waist height.

"Well," she said. "You really are a mess, aren't you?"

The broken man did not respond. Kiko pulled an octopus of wires loose from a ring on the wall, checked the ends, then set about tying the man up just in case he woke. She bound his wrists and ankles and gave a good tug on the knots to check that they were tight.

Now that they were inside, Kiko began to regret her decision. Fancy trousers aside, he was human. He did not belong here. It would not have been so bad if he had been dead, truly broken beyond repair. Then it would have been all right. The stars would have eaten him. The meat would not have been wasted. His clothing could have gone to the market to be remade and sold back to someone in the cloud city. But he was not dead, and although Kiko knew humans were destructive, selfish creatures, she did not want to be responsible for letting the man die.

She pulled the half-empty pot from the warmer and poured herself a mug of the sour, oily brew. She would take him to the market in the morning, she decided. She would give him to Osaka, who would remake him, and then he would go back to the cloud city, and she could go back to gathering her plastics. She had done her part when she brought him in here instead of leaving him for the stars and the radiation. As long as no-one found him here and knew that she had picked him illegally, it would be fine.

She opened her collecting basket and fished out what she had gathered that morning. It was not a lot. The man had distracted her. She sorted what little she had into piles, then dumped the pieces into the scrubber and set it going. It would clean and soften the plastics, ready to be traded at the market. She needed a new battery for her coolers, and her food supplies were running low.

When the scrubber had finished, Kiko weighed her haul.

She had known it would be bad, but not that bad. Her heart sank as she opened the door to her workshop and looked outside, wondering if she had time to go out for more. But the sun was too high, heating the island and sending the gas levels up. The meter on her suit showed orange. She let go of the door.

It didn't close fast enough. Riak was outside. He bounced over in his neon haz suit, sun reflecting off his wide helmet with its ridiculous feather plumes. "Kiko," he called. "Hey, Kiko!" He caught the edge of the door in one gloved hand and shoved it back up. What could kill a star unfortunately could not chop through Riak's left hand quite so easily.

"Riak," she said, politely, carefully.

"What's going on?" he asked, tilting his wide head from side to side, trying to see past her and into the workshop. His arm was locked rigid against the weight of the door. He wasn't much taller than Kiko, but he was twice as wide and strong, his cartilaginous joints reinforced by the plastic that had seeped into them.

"Nothing," she said, pushing out a hip and setting a hand to it, spreading herself as wide as she could, hoping he'd take the hint and leave.

"Not like you to have the door up during scorch hours. Dangerous for a girl like you to be exposed to this."

"Then you should move and let me shut the door."

"I'm only being friendly," he said, his voice dangerously soft. "Met your quota today?"

Kiko said nothing.

"You know, if you were a little nicer to me, I might find a way to help you top up your load. I've already got mine."

She eyed the counter where she kept her trusty weapon, an arm-length bat fashioned from a discarded steel pole wrapped with fishing string. She'd loaded the end with chunks of concrete, giving it a hefty weight. It wouldn't kill Riak, but it would put a good dent in his head. "No thanks."

Riak clacked his teeth at her, snap snap snap, and then he shrugged and wandered off, the feathers on his stupid helmet bobbing up and down. Kiko dropped the door and only wished that Riak's foot or perhaps some smaller, softer part of him had been under it when it fell. But alas. Such things were only dreams. She had to focus on reality, on what was and what could be.

If she was caught with the man in her workshop, she would be kicked off the island and into the sea, and she definitely did not want to spend the rest of her life swimming in that toxic soup. She was a fool. She should have left the man where she'd found him.

She would have to take him to the market at first light. Riak didn't start picking until midday. But how best to transport him? She rummaged through a box, found enough sheets of plastic to knot together into a cape to cover the man. If she took him early and then came back and worked hard, she would be able to catch up her shortfall from today, and everything would be fine. It would be as if the man had never been here. But he was here, and she found herself talking to him, even though he did not talk back.

"I know you have been inside Orenda's machine," she confessed. "I snuck into his workshop one day at the market so I could see it. A man climbed inside, an ordinary human man. It thundered and roared." She wrinkled her nose as the memory came back. "It smelled like boiling meat. When they took him out, he was beautiful. Glistening black skin and emerald green hair. I had never seen anything so magnificent. Sometimes I wonder what it would be like to be remade. To be new and beautiful. But trash pickers cannot use the machine. When we are broken, it is done. We are not valuable enough to repair. But you are. If I take you to the market and put you back into the machine, will that fix you?" She didn't want him to die. He was young, and it would be a waste of healthy flesh and potential.

The chime of the clock on the wall told her that it was getting late. Her empty stomachs reminded that she had not eaten all day. There was only a single dried kelpcake and half a loaf of saltbread left. She looked at the bread, and she looked at the man. She ate half and saved half, in case the man woke up and was hungry.

She gave him a blanket, a patchwork of pink and blue that she had made herself, and tucked it round his broken body, then she settled down to watch him. She did not think she would sleep, until she found herself waking up, curled up on the floor, confused and stiff. She thought that the man had been a dream, until she saw him in the corner of her workshop.

He was still asleep. Humans were *lazy*.

She loaded her scrap and the man onto her speedbike. It took three tries to power up the engine, and the weight of the man made it slow and noisy. It took them twice as long as normal to reach the market, and by the time they did, Kiko was exhausted. Her mouth was parched. She spent what coin she had on a bag of water. She watched the little ships streaming down from the city, coming to collect their bundles of salvaged plastics, that they would make into more bags and wrappers and then throw away. Orenda's was already busy. There was a human woman inside, short and round with waist-length curls of glossy black hair. She had a tidy nose and a poisonous expression, and her eyebrows were etched so sharply onto her face that they looked as if they could cut. Her dress was red, as was her coat and her hat and her pointed shoes. She was haggling with Orenda. Kiko did not stop to hear the terms. Better to take advantage of the fact that the workshop was empty. She considered simply leaving the man outside the shop, but then her mind played through a hundred ways that could go wrong, and she frightened herself out of it. She had put too much effort into bringing him here for him to not be repaired.

The machine was housed in a workshop at the side of Orenda's shop. It was magnificent, a strange and wondrous thing two metres tall and two metres wide, built from sheets of hammered metal, the outside laced with silver and gold wire. It was an ancient technology, something from the time before the cloud city, and only Orenda knew how it worked. But Kiko knew enough to pull open the door and somehow lift the man inside, pushing his arms and legs out of the way before closing it. She had to lean her full weight against it to get the lock to catch. But catch it did, and she pressed the buttons on the side of the machine as she had seen Orenda do.

Then she stepped back. She knew she should leave, that she might get caught, but she was suddenly desperate to know how the man turned out, if the machine could actually repair someone rather than just change them. She wanted to see him made new.

The machine thundered and whirred, purple steam hissing through the edge of the door. It made her cough. Then came the banging and the smell like boiled meat. All was as it had been before. She had been worried that she had not pressed the buttons in the right combination, that she might have done something wrong, but her worry lessened at the familiar signs.

The lights flashed and then they went off and it was done. She tugged open the door and the man fell out. Kiko grabbed him under the arms and tried to get him to his feet, but he was big and unsteady.

But he was alive.

He was alive.

"You..." he said, and came crashing towards her, his eyes flickering from silver to lilac to yellow to blue. He sank to his knees, bracing his weight on his hands, and looked up at her.

Kiko staggered back, suddenly terrified. He had not

seemed so frightening when he was unconscious and silent and pliable, but he was frightening now. His skin was dark pewter, his eyes and hair an identical shade of deepest emerald green. All of him was flesh. There were no ugly pieces of plastic, no crumpled, awkward angles to his body. It was too much for Kiko.

She turned, meaning to run out of the workshop, and made it as far as the door.

But she did not make it out of the door.

"Hello," said Riak, his wide mouth curving. "What are you doing in here?"

He sauntered into the workshop, forcing Kiko to back up. "I knew you were up to something," he said. She could taste his rancid breath tainting the air. "You're in so much trouble." Too late, she saw the movement of his left pincer. There was no way to avoid it. It clamped hard down on her arm, slicing straight through the jelly-soft flesh.

Kiko clutched at the wound. Fluid poured from it, puddling at her feet as she stared at Riak in disbelief. She staggered back as behind her, the man snapped to his feet. In one smooth movement, he grabbed her by the arm, pulled her out of the way, and punched Riak right in the throat gills, sending him sprawling.

Her arm burned as if Riak had lit a fire inside it, and somehow Kiko knew that if she did not stop the gush of fluid, she would die. She could already feel her strength beginning to fade. In front of her, the two men continued to fight. Behind her was the machine.

Kiko turned and looked at it. The little door was open. Could she? She glanced back at the others, and in that moment her mind was made up. She pushed the buttons with her good hand and then threw herself inside, clattering to the bottom. It was cold and wet. She was too shocked to scream, too shocked to do anything, and then the machine began to turn, and she was spun round and round. Her body was heated to a temperature she felt sure would end everything. She was being cooked from the inside out. She pressed her hands against the inside of the drum, but they were no longer her hands, she was nothing, she was gone; the stink of boiled meat and burning plastic rose up around her and she choked it down, knowing it came from her body.

And then everything went dark.

She did not remember being removed from the machine. She did not remember anything until she awoke in a soft white room that was not her own. She staggered to the doorway, her body strange, and out onto a sweeping balcony. The moisture of the cloud touched her face as she fell against the balustrade and slumped over it, looking down. The island spread out below her, though she could only see pieces of it when the moisture parted enough to let her.

She was in the cloud city.

She crawled back into the room and stretched out on the bed, tired, so tired. She did not know how long she slept. When she awoke, her body still felt wrong, but the shock of it was less. Her hands were the palest shade of green. Her fingers were long and elegant. She touched her face and didn't recognise it. She found a mirror and looked at herself.

The scales on her legs were silver and shimmering and beautiful, her gill slits now only a pattern on her skin. Her body had lost its softness and instead she was firm and opaque and *real*. She looked exotic and wonderful, not a trash picker, not a creature that had come from the sea, but like something that belonged up here.

The room had a door. It took some time to figure out how to open it, but she got there in the end and, feeling terribly pleased with herself, she stepped out into a long corridor. There were more doors, so many doors, and everything was so clean. Not a fingerprint to smudge any of the surfaces. She caught the scent of food, and followed it. She found herself in a vast room filled with tables and chairs and people, all new and shiny and perfect. A man hurried over. "A seat, madame, a seat," he said, and led her to a table.

There were other people already sat at it. Kiko recognised the woman from Orenda's, with her sausage curls and spiteful face, though the others were strangers to her. She watched them, folding her new body into a seat in the same way that they did. Then the food arrived. It was unlike anything she'd had before.

Everything was fresh. Her mouth watered at the taste of it. The first portion was so generous that it was too much for her, but still the food kept coming. Plates were whisked away barely touched. She noticed that the others didn't even bother to try most of what was placed in front of them, too busy talking to take much notice of it.

There was no sign of the man. Kiko wondered what had happened to him, if he was even here. She wanted to leave the table and try to find him, but she did not dare move until the others did so.

It was the woman with the curled hair who spoke to her first. "I'm sorry," she said, her voice sugar sweet. "Who are you?"

Kiko shrank back into her seat, suddenly very afraid. She said the first thing that came into her head. Her own name. "I'm Kiko."

"Kiko?" The woman laughed, but there was no humour in it. "What an odd name. I don't believe we've met."

Did she suspect? Did she know that Kiko was a trash picker, made from the fish and the plastic and the poison, that she did not belong up here in the cloud city?

"We met once," Kiko lied. "It was a long time ago."

"Did we? I am sure I would remember. I am usually so good with names." She leaned in, as if she intended to question Kiko further, but then someone else swaggered in, tall and huge with devil-red skin and eyes of pure black. He was so magnificent that Kiko felt a little overwhelmed. At least she understood now why no-one had questioned her scales. Up here, she was not unusual at all.

"Dexter, you devil!" squealed the curly-haired woman, and the others joined in, and Kiko was soon forgotten. She was no longer new and interesting. The others clapped and cheered as Dexter flexed and showed off his new body. They would have a party, they declared. It would be that night. Everyone was invited. They must celebrate Dexter's remaking. Wasn't he magnificent! Such a bold choice!

Others talked of his new red skin. There was envy in their tone, even though to Kiko they all looked equally as impressive as

Dexter, some even more so. She was pulled into the crowd and went with them as they planned for the party. Everyone needed new clothes, new shoes. They went through all the shops, exchanging piles of silver coin for trinkets. Each one was hidden inside layers of paper and cardboard and plastic, as if its newness would somehow slip away if it were left exposed to the air. As they went from shop to shop, Kiko began to realise that what these people wanted, what they really wanted, was what they did not yet possess. The joy lived only in the moments between seeing something and buying it.

The time for the party soon came around. A great show was made of dressing, as many new outfits were declared unsuitable and thrown aside. The others downed a great deal of a dark liquid that they called wine, and grew louder with each mouthful.

It was impossible to tell where the preparation ended and the party truly began as they moved together in a loud, scented rabble to another building, this one even more magnificent. It had been decorated specially for the event. Everything matched Dexter's new skin.

At first, Kiko found all of this rather exciting, but that soon started to fade. The wine made her feel sick, and it was almost impossible to stop herself from picking through the discarded wrappings that littered the floor. She crawled back to her apartment and lay down on the bed and fell asleep. When she awoke, it was morning. The sun was up and the sky was new, and she washed herself and ate a simple breakfast in her room. She was soon encouraged out by the others, who wanted to go shopping.

"But you went shopping yesterday," Kiko said. "Do you not have what you need?"

They all laughed at her. "Kiko," they said. "You are so funny."

They went shopping. More coin was handed over, and there were more trinkets wrapped in a dozen layers to protect their newness. To Kiko, they looked just like the ones they had bought yesterday. She could not see the difference. She said as much, and they laughed some more and called her a tease.

One of the men reappeared, and he was as red as Dexter, and there was a fight. Kiko turned away. Everything here was so different to life on the island. No-one up here wanted for anything. No-one had to wait for anything. Nothing had any real value. They told each other and themselves that they were happy, but Kiko could not see it. They all seemed trapped in a cycle of utter misery.

Before, when she had been on the island, she had looked up to the cloud city and thought how wonderful it would be to live up here, to have a life where everything was new, where there was more than enough of everything.

It was not wonderful.

But she could not leave. She was trapped. She didn't know how to work the little ships that went down to the surface, and she was afraid to ask the others to help. The group claimed to be friends and were constantly declaring their love for each other, yet they were jealous and covetous and secretive and possessive. If one bought a blue jewel, and then another also bought a blue jewel, the first blue jewel would be thrown away amid shouting and tears. They kept cupboards full of things that they had no use for, but refused to share them.

A few days later, at the end of another party, after another fight and too much sweet wine, conversation turned to a man called Lock. They wondered where he had gone. There was talk of missing him, though it did not seem real to Kiko, just a new emotion to try out and play with. They had not missed him when they had been shopping and drinking and partying.

"What happened to him?" she asked.

"Fell from the tower," said one of the others.

"The fool," said the curly-haired woman, who was now tall and thin, with very white skin and very white hair. "Why bother with the tower? Why not just have himself remade, if he was so bored?"

"Perhaps he did not want to be remade," Kiko said. "Perhaps he knew that it would not help."

This time, the laughter was stilted. No-one told her she was funny.

She left the party, and went in search of the tower. It was

not difficult to find. There were many steps to the top, and when she reached it, she was above the clouds. She was above it all, and there was nowhere left to go but down. She did not want to stay here in the cloud city, where things were new and then they were old and there was nothing in between. She climbed up onto the wall that ringed the edge of the tower. She looked out at the sky, drenched dark by night, and knew why the man called Lock had come here.

Falling was easy. Landing was hard. She crashed into a mountain of tangled copper wires and green computer chips and old phones and lay there, completely broken.

But it was not the end, for someone had been waiting for Kiko.

He found her there, in that pile of tangled copper wires. He pulled her free and loaded her onto the back of a scooter weighed down with white plastic bottles. He took her to the market. He was smart, this man of the city. He understood that there was another way, a better way, that what had once been broken could be repaired, that there was something in between being new and being old.

Orenda took one look at Lock's jewelled glove and pronounced it to be priceless. Lock sold it to him for a tumble in the machine. He placed Kiko carefully into the drum, and Orenda closed the door and set the programme running. There was nothing Lock could do but sit and wait as it thundered and belched and made a smell like boiled meat.

At last, it was done.

Orenda opened the door and left, his part of the bargain fulfilled.

Lock held his breath. He was almost too frightened to approach, but he forced himself to do it. He did not know what she had become, the woman of the island and of the city. He only hoped that she was alive. He did not dare to hope for more.

He pulled her out of the machine and held her in his arms and whispered to her. "Kiko," he said. "Kiko, wake up."

Her eyes fluttered open, and his heart skipped a beat. They were not like the other eyes he had seen. They did not flicker from colour to colour, a remnant of every time she had been new. They were the same colour, the same solid yellow with a sharp horizontal pupil slashed across the centre. Those eyes looked up at him, and he saw confusion and recognition. "You," she said. "How?"

"I found you," Lock told her. "I brought you to the market and put you in the machine."

"Why?"

"You were broken, and you needed to be repaired."

"I fell," Kiko told him. "I could not bear it, and so I fell."

"I know," Lock told her.

"The city is wrong. I thought it would be paradise, but it is not. It is misery. No-one there is happy. They cannot be content with what they have. All that interests them is what they do not have, and it comes to them so easily that when they get it, it brings them no joy. It is a poison. How do they survive it? How?"

"Because they live in ignorance. It is easier than facing the truth." He helped her to her feet, and together they staggered out of Orenda's workshop. "They are all empty. Their lives are empty. They keep using, keep consuming, telling themselves that one day, the void will be filled. But how can they ever be full when they throw everything away?"

Outside, the market was familiar, in sound and colour and smell. Lock wasn't sure he would ever get used to it, but it no longer frightened him. He had accepted that it was not something he could escape from.

"How do I look?" Kiko asked him then.

"Like... yourself," he told her, and smiled, and she smiled back at him.

"That is good enough."

They returned to the workshop. Lock had to drive the scootbike. It was old and battered and the paint was scratched. It was the sort of bike that had been popular in the city maybe five years before. No-one had a bike like this now. And yet it worked, and if the ride was uncomfortable, it was because of him, not because of the machine. He vowed to take the time to learn how to ride it properly.

At the workshop, Kiko rolled up the door and walked inside, and he saw the way her shoulders relaxed when she found herself home. She did not need more than this. It was enough. That was the moment when Lock fell in love with Kiko. He had felt the edges of it before, but it had not been a real, fully formed thing. Now it was. It had woken up and surrounded him, and over the next few days, it surrounded her too. They wore it like the softest of cloaks, reaching out to touch it occasionally, but otherwise happy to just feel the weight of it and know it was there.

She taught him to gather the plastics and clean them. Every day more of them rained down from the cloud city. Lock did not like it. As he waded through another pool of discarded bags, he could not understand why there were so many. What were they for, he asked himself. What had been in them? There was no way of knowing.

And Lock began to plan.

He shared his idea with Kiko, but it was too new and it was not ready, so every day they took it out and added to it, until it was just right. They wove ropes from the bags, thick as his leg and ten times as strong. When the time was right, Lock took the ropes up to the city. He fastened them to the walls, to the tower, and threw the trailing ends down to the island below. The others laughed and told him he was funny, but they did not try to stop him. He was different to them now. He thought of Kiko, waiting for him down below. Slowly, the crabs wove the ends of the ropes into the island, blissfully unaware of what they did.

And then, one day, the crabs wove the ropes in that last little bit.

When the island began to warm, and the gases began to rise, the ropes shrank in on themselves, growing shorter and shorter, pulling on the cloud city until all those who lived in it fell into the mess of their own making. It buried the market and broke Orenda's machine.

The people from the city came out and picked their way through the filth of the island, shrieking in horror. They were no longer able to deny what they had created. There would be no escape from it now.

Lock ran straight to Kiko.

"We broke the city," Kiko said.

Lock smiled down at her. "Good," he said. "Now we have a chance to repair it."

SPACE ROCKS

Kerry Buchanan

An alarm blared, breaking into Inge's cryo-sleep dreams, bringing her back to consciousness with a pounding heart. She took a deep, shuddering breath of stale air, then opened her eyes as her plexiglass capsule cracked open, releasing sleep gases into the stasis bay.

Bloody cabin smells worse than the sulphur planet.

The klaxon still sounded its urgent summons to action for the ship's captain, always the first to wake. She arched her back, filling her lungs with air that was slightly fresher than the capsule's. A ding and a hiss announced that Agba, her navigation officer, wouldn't be too far behind.

With limbs like spaghetti, Inge clambered out of the capsule, steadied herself on the canopy for a moment, then made a staggering run for the door. It opened with a soft ping, letting her through onto the corridor that ran the length of the ship.

Once on the bridge, she gave a deep sigh of relief: Earth filled the viewing screen, a swirling mass of blues and greens with whirlpool clouds. So familiar, and so much more beautiful than any of the other places they'd seen in the last few years. But the alarm still blared out, so she tore her eyes from her home planet and checked the flashing lights on the console.

Blasted hold alarm again. Ben was supposed to have fixed that. It had been going off at intervals before they set off on the long journey home, but it must have been a faulty sensor, because whenever they checked the hold, it seemed fine, with no sign of the cargo shifting. So many systems on this old vessel were showing their age now. Maybe it was a good thing it was her last voyage.

She slapped the button on the main console to shut off the noise, then sank into her command chair, letting it mould around her body.

The bridge doors pinged open, and Inge spun her chair to watch Agba as he lurched in, clinging to the doorframe just as Inge had a moment ago. He stared at the viewing screen, then smiled as he saw Earth floating just where it should be. "We're home."

"How many missions has it been now, Agba?" Inge said, smiling as she checked the readouts. "And you're still mildly surprised when your navigation brings us home." There was no malice in her words. They had been a team now for nearly twenty years, and their trust in each other had survived all the tests that long-term missions threw at them.

Agba shook his head, almost overbalancing, then wobbled his way to the nav station to check their position manually. Inge watched him while she waited for the others to wake, savouring the moment. This would almost certainly be their last voyage together. Last time they were home, Inge had requested reassignment to Earth to spend some time with Haredd, her life-partner.

The other two came onto the bridge together. Ben, her co-pilot, and Stephanie, the mission's scientific officer. Stephanie held Ben's hand, pulling him forwards, ending up standing just a little too close to Agba, who frowned as his fingers flew across the console.

"We made it!" Stephanie said, stating the obvious. "Well done, Agba." She patted him on the shoulder. "We'll make a navigator of you yet."

"What's our status, Agba?" Inge asked, trying to put

Stephanie out of her mind.

"Just coming into orbital range, Skipper. Estimate two Earth hours and we'll be ready to hook up with Bloody Mary." The International Space Station had earned the nickname due to the bright red algal bloom that coated its surface, as well as its shape, reminiscent of a tightly-corseted woman from the twenty-third century. "I doubt if they'll hold us long in quarantine."

"Good work," Inge said, and was rewarded by a shy smile and a duck of Agba's head.

The comms unit buzzed into life. "This is Houston Control to the craft entering orbital range."

Ben slipped into the seat beside Inge to answer. "Houston Control, this is Bravo Foxtrot Golf Seven Niner Seven requesting clearance to dock."

"Greetings, Seven Niner Seven, and welcome home." Haredd had made certain she was on comms for their return, and the familiar husky voice warmed Inge. Haredd's voice dropped, making her next words seem personal. "We've missed you all."

Inge's chest constricted. *Home.* It took a couple of deep breaths before she could be sure of her voice to answer. "It's good to be back, Houston Control." She cleared her throat. "No living organisms to declare. Just some rock samples."

"Some pretty unique rock samples," Stephanie butted in, ignoring protocol. "I'd say there'll be a research paper in this lot."

There was an uncomfortable silence for a moment, then the voice of Colonel Fitzpatrick, the base commander, rang out through the cockpit speakers. "Bravo Foxtrot Golf Seven Niner Seven, take up a Q position at the outer marker until you're cleared by the medibots."

"Acknowledged, sir," Ben said, his voice tight with embarrassment. "Taking up position."

The hull vibrated slightly as the thrusters kicked in, shuffling them into their holding pattern. This was always the worst part of the journey – so close to home, but so far away. The waiting seemed interminable.

Half a dozen specks appeared in the distance, rocketing towards them. The small robots circled the ship so fast they became streaks as they passed the viewing screen. Inge split the screen and activated the external cameras so they could watch the progress of the scan.

The bots reached the far end of the ship and began again, slightly slower this time. Inge forced her face into a neutral expression, but her hands slid on the metal arms of her chair, slippery with sweat.

"Why's it taking so long?" Stephanie asked.

"It always feels like this," Ben reassured her. "Nothing to worry about."

But Inge had been asking herself the same question. Now the bots had congregated at the aft end of the hull, outside the main hold. Exactly where Stephanie had stored the rock samples. Then they began a rapid and complex dance, appearing as streams of light enclosing the whole ship in a glowing net.

"Do they usually do that?" Stephanie asked, her voice high-pitched.

Inge's stomach cramped in fear. She had seen this happen only once before, and it hadn't ended well for the crew.

"This is Houston Control to Bravo Foxtrot Golf Seven Niner Seven." This time the voice was clipped and official – and not one she recognised. "You have been declared a potential bio-hazard. Prepare to be boarded and inspected."

The blood drained from Agba's and Ben's faces, but Stephanie's flushed an ugly red.

"Easy, Steph." Inge reached out to touch the younger woman's arm. "It'll be a mistake, you wait. Those bots are getting on in years, you know."

Stephanie slapped Inge's hand away. "Don't talk down to me! I'm no rookie, and I understand exactly what this means." Her voice cracked.

Ben stood and tried to take Stephanie in his arms, but she pushed him away, hard enough for him to fall onto the sharp corner of the console.

"That's enough." Inge allowed a touch of the authority she rarely needed to creep into her voice. "Everyone, take your places and check all our systems. It could be we've had a circuit board fried and we're sending out the wrong information." All three of them stared back with hope in their faces and she felt like a traitor, but at least this would keep their minds occupied.

The customs vessel pulled alongside two hours later. A ponderous craft, it was only designed for short hops carrying cargo and troops.

"Prepare your boarding hatch," an invisible voice commanded.

Ben turned on the floodlights to light up the outer skin, so the customs officers could see the hatch. A telescopic boarding tunnel crept out across the intervening space, clamping on to their steel hull with a clang that echoed even as far as the bridge. The ship shuddered, and Inge stroked the console as if soothing a fretful horse.

An indicator lit up on the instrument panel as the heavily-suited inspection party entered the companionway, boots echoing on the steel steps. Inge counted eight of them in all – too many to fit on the ship's tiny bridge. "Stay here," she instructed. "I'll meet them and see if I can get this cleared up quickly."

Stephanie jumped to her feet. "How do we know we can trust you? Maybe you'll make some sort of deal, and leave us here."

Ben gasped and Agba's eyes widened.

Inge made herself smile. "If you really think, after all these months working together, that I'm capable of that, why not listen in on the comm channel and watch us on the cameras?"

"I will." Stephanie flicked her ponytail back over her shoulder as she spun to glare at the two men. "And don't pretend it hadn't crossed your minds, too. I'm just the only one with the cojones to say it."

Inge turned her back on her crew and began the long walk down towards the hatch. Steel gantries whispered as her soft shoes trod steadily forwards, but after a few minutes she saw a light bobbing towards her.

"Ahoy, boarding party! Captain Inge Collier here. Welcome aboard."

"Hello, Captain," a cultured voice replied, slightly distorted by the helmet. "Major Foster from Houston Control. Sorry about all this. Most unpleasant."

"Unpleasant is an understatement, but you're only doing your job, Major Foster. Where do you want to start?"

"Probably the bridge and work backwards to the area the bots indicated," the major said. "But we'll split into teams to get through this as quickly as possible."

"I appreciate that, Major. Let me know if there's anything my crew or I can do to help."

"Well, actually, I'd quite like a word with your scientific officer, if I may? I was reading your records on the way over here and it seems she was a late replacement on the crew. Not terribly experienced, I gather?"

Inge mentally kicked herself for suggesting Stephanie should listen in. Too late to worry now. "Certainly. Follow me, sir."

By the time they reached the bridge, Stephanie had gone from angry to incandescent. She faced up to the major, standing on tip-toes to glare through his face-plate. "How *dare* you suggest any of this is *my* fault?"

Inge might have been amused, under better conditions, to note that she actually spat like a cat, leaving tiny balls of spittle on the plexiglass.

"This old wreck of a research vessel is probably malfunctioning everywhere, but the Council can't be seen to be cutting corners, can they? So some poor sucker has to take the blame. Well, it won't be me. I'm no scapegoat."

The major swayed back slightly. When Stephanie paused for breath, he cut in. "Would the rest of you please go to your individual quarters until called? I will be speaking to each of you in turn."

Inge herded the other two off the bridge ahead of her. Before the door closed behind her, she heard the major say, "Now, Doctor Jess. I was hoping that, as scientific officer, you would be able to help us. Where do you think we should start looking for the problem?"

Clever man, she thought. *Spiking Stephanie's guns.*

#

Lying in her small cabin with her hands behind her head, Inge studied the ceiling. In all the years she'd lived on this ship she'd never spent so long in this small space: not awake, anyway. Her mind kept turning over the same questions – and coming up blank each time. She'd tried to dictate a message to Haredd, but the words had refused to come. She knew she should feel something, some grief for what might have been, but her mind kept on swinging back to Stephanie and Ben.

But how could they have picked up contamination? They had been doing this job as a team for so long now, they all knew every routine inside out. *Except Stephanie*, a small, treacherous voice whispered. *I've seen her take shortcuts.*

Stephanie was a skilled scientific officer, with dozens of successes to her name. Inge had checked her out thoroughly before bringing her along with them, and she had come highly recommended by her previous captain, who had given her a glowing reference. Had the reference had been *too* glowing? The final gambit of an officer who wanted rid of an unpopular crewmember?

Inge's name boomed over the intercom, bringing a not-unwelcome end to her negative thoughts. The others had already been called, one by one, then returned to their own cabins, feet dragging on the checker-plate floors as they passed her door.

When she reached the bridge, the major was sitting in the command chair, but he rose to his feet and indicated that she should take it. Instead, he sank into the co-pilot's seat, stretching long legs out in front of him.

"Captain Collier. *Inge*. Please, can you talk me through the routines you and your crew used throughout this mission? Others in my team are processing your log, but I'd like to hear it in your own words, please."

For the next half hour or so, he questioned her about their procedures: the protective suits they wore, and the way their suits and all other materials were decontaminated. She answered him concisely and honestly.

At last he stopped, and the silence lengthened, broken only by the soft sound of his ventilation pack. Inge gripped the arms of her chair. Was he receiving information from his other teams? Was that why he'd fallen silent? Somehow, she knew what was coming before he spoke.

"Inge. I really am terribly sorry about this, but my team's equipment has confirmed life signs in your main hold."

The metal arms dug into the palms of her hands as she gripped them convulsively. She made herself relax, loosening her fingers. "Life signs?" She knew she sounded stupid, but what else could she say? There couldn't be any life signs. They had been so careful, had followed every protocol.

"Yes." The major rose to his feet. "In fact, since we sent the scanning robots into the hold, the team have been picking up some unusual noises, too." He leaned across her and flicked the switch for the speakers in the main hold. "Can you hear me?"

For a moment, Inge thought it might be an ill-timed joke, but then a sound blasted out across the bridge, a high-pitched squealing that might have been animal in origin, except there was also something harsh and gravelly about it.

"My second-in-command believes it possible that they might understand us," Foster said. "But I'm not so sure, and if this is their attempt at a reply, it's not a form of speech I've ever come across before."

Hysterical laughter tried to bubble up from inside Inge, but she took a deep breath and managed to nod encouragingly.

"As soon as the noises began, I withdrew my team and sealed the hold. They're on their way up here now, but I believe you have remote cameras in there, don't you?"

Did he really not know, or was this an attempt to make her feel useful? Inge cleared her throat. "We do. I'll activate them." She toggled the switches up and down a few times until a burst of static flashed on the viewing screen. "Sorry. The old girl can be a bit temperamental sometimes." After a moment, a picture started to come through. "Haven't used the hold cameras in a while," she said. "We're only carrying rocks – or so we thought."

The walls at the far side of the hold came into view,

showing stacked packing crates and the lift-trolley they used planet-side. Some of the crates were tipped over, the rocks Stephanie had collected littered around them.

"I don't understand," Inge said. "We had those well secured before we set off." She remembered, with a guilty pang, the alarm that had woken her from stasis and had been going off occasionally before that. Couldn't give Stephanie the blame for that, either, because as captain, Inge should have checked it out herself instead of relying on Ben.

Then one of the rocks rolled a little until it bounced off another, bigger one. The noise she'd heard through the intercom broke out again, but now she could see what was happening, she thought she could distinguish two distinct pitches, almost as if two different voices were speaking. She strained to see where the sounds were coming from, but there was nothing in the hold except the tumbled crates and the rocks.

Inge's Scandinavian blood had given her an interest in the myths and legends of her ancestors' land, and a tiny flicker of recognition tried to flare up as she watched the rock moving across the floor. She tightened her lips and pushed the distraction away. That was ancient Norway, not her lovely modern universe with its Galactic Council and space research programmes.

But there was no doubt that they had discovered something, out there in the uncharted galaxies. Her mouth was dry with excitement. They had been searching for sentient life for so long, coming up blank every time. Could this be it? Stephanie's name would be famous, and they'd never hear the end of it.

"Can you hear me?" she asked into the microphone.

Several more rocks rolled across the floor, until they were loosely gathered together, rather like a group of strangers waiting for a shuttle. One of them, bigger than the others, rolled forward. It moved towards the camera, almost as though it knew it was being watched.

"Squeee. Squeee squee."

This time, the sound was piercingly loud and high-pitched. Inge put her fingers in her ears, wincing.

"What the hell was that?" Ben asked from the doorway.

"Sorry, Major Foster, but we could hear that awful noise from our cabins, and we had to come and see what was happening." Behind him, Agba and Stephanie craned to see, their eyes glued to the viewing screen.

Another blast of noise threatened to deafen them. Inge turned the volume down, making it almost bearable. The large rock had moved back to join the others, and it occurred to her that they were conversing amongst themselves now. The flicker of recognition was stronger now, refusing to be dismissed.

"Hold on," Ben said. "Can I see, please, Major?" The major stood up to let Ben sit in the co-pilot's seat. His fingers flew over the controls again. "I think I might be able to do something with the noise. Stephanie, can you run that linguistics programme you were working on, if I. Just. Do. This..." He tapped in one last command.

Stephanie tapped away at her own terminal, mumbling under her breath. "Ready," she said. "Try speaking to them now."

"Can you hear me?" Inge asked again, but this time it came out of the bridge speakers as a squeal, making her jump. She exchanged a glance with Agba, but he just shrugged, eyes alert.

On the screen, all the rocks began to move, almost vibrating. The biggest – the Spokesrock, Inge thought irreverently – bounced once on the steel floor. It made a deep booming noise and immediately the others all stopped moving, shuffling back into their original formation.

"Yes," a deep voice echoed through the speakers, slurred but intelligible. "Hearing you now. Understanding."

"Allah preserve us," Agba said in a hushed voice. "Did you hear that?"

"Shh!" Ben, Stephanie and Inge all said at the same time.

"Sorry to cause fear," the rock said. "Wanted to go home."

I shouldn't really go on calling them rocks, Inge thought. *Not when they're clearly sentient.* But the only other name she could think of for them had too many bad connotations; too many links with the myths of her land.

"Home?" the major asked, sounding hassled for the first time since he'd come aboard. "That might not be possible."

The rock rotated a little, swaying where it sat. "This is home," it said. "Been gone long, long time."

"Wait – you mean Earth is your home?" That was Stephanie, taking the words out of Inge's mouth. Inge held her breath, the flicker catching and burning with added fuel from memories of whispered stories in the Academy.

"Earth is home."

"I don't understand," Stephanie said, frowning. "We found you light years from here. How can Earth possibly be your home?"

"Sent away," the rock said. "Punished. Want home now. Be good."

Oh no. Inge's stomach knotted up, and a buzzing began in her head that had nothing to do with the rocks' voices. She'd begun to remember more of the stories that had been passed between trainees in the Academy, the ones no one dared speak out loud. Just another conspiracy theory, Inge had always thought.

"What did you do to deserve exile?" Stephanie asked eagerly.

She won't have heard the stories. She trained at the Science College, not the Academy. She tried to work moisture into her mouth.

"Ate hoomans," the rock replied without hesitation. "Gal-ac-tic Coun-cil sent us into exile. Know better now. Ready to come home."

"*What* are you?" Stephanie asked, glowing with self-importance. It must have just dawned on her that they'd brought back a new species, new to present-day Earth at any rate.

But if Inge was right, they were all in serious trouble, even more trouble than they'd guessed at when the bots scanned them for life signs. The stories told of a species that had all but wiped out mankind; but that had been over a thousand years ago, if it had ever happened at all. Of course, the location of their exile planet had been a well-guarded secret – too well guarded, perhaps, if her crew had stumbled upon it.

"We Rock-Trolls," the rock said, and Inge imagined she heard pride in its voice.

"Oh shit." The major slammed his hand down on the red

button on the main console, sending the warning klaxon screaming through the ship.

"Houston Control, we have a problem...."

THE ICE MAN

Rosie Oliver

The on-duty alarm kicked Soldis out of her instantly forgettable dream, into that not-quite-there half sleep. Her hand fumbled its way from under the bedclothes to flick the alarm off, and whipped back into the nestled warmth.

"What do you want?" she moaned into her pillow.

"Get your butt in here pronto," a raspy male voice yelled out of the tiny speaker. "We've caught a murder."

She cut off her groan and sat bolt upright, letting her duvet fold down in front of her. The cool bedroom air stung her skin, which pushed her into focussing. "Here? In Kiruna?"

"Yes. Can you confirm face recog?"

The voice was now identifiable: Arne Hjalmar, the town's police chief. She yanked her phone from its stand to hold its screen in front of her, and finger-stabbed the blue "F" key.

"Face recog accepted," its tenor voice announced.

The screen switched to a picture of a naked woman thrown across a ridge of snow at the side of a concrete path. Muscle-tight due to youth and exercise, she was thin enough that Soldis could count the ribs down her back. Her face was turned away, hair splayed out on the snow. Its strawberry-blonde shade was very unusual for this part of Sweden. Either she was a tourist or she visited an expensive hairdresser. Yet the shade was familiar. Soldis tried to recall where she had last seen it.

An "H" in the picture's top right corner indicated this was a slice through a holograph, taken by a holo-drone as standard procedure. She rotated the bi-gimbal ring that controlled her view to "fly" a curved path to come face to face with the victim.

Soldis yelped, dropped her phone and placed her hand over her mouth, sickness rising in her throat.

"First time seeing a murder victim?" Arne said in disgust.

She swallowed her bile. "No," she croaked, and coughed. "It's Anneka Engdahl, a friend from school days."

"Oh hell! Are you still close friends?"

"No." She was better than this squeamish doing-the-tasks-by-rote policewoman, so she took a couple of deep breaths: get the facts recorded. "I lost contact with her nine years ago when she went off to Lund University to study biochemistry."

"Good. I'm short-staffed as it is. Get here soonest." The phone clicked dead.

#

Soldis had to force her way into the small, crowded-with-too-much-kit-squeezed-in operations room, and inwardly cursed Arne for calling her last. She shouldered her way round the back to find a gap to stare at the wall-screen. Kiruna's street map had a red cross behind Bjorkplan, undoubtedly where Anneka's body had been found. The marked-off blocks around it meant door-to-door enquiries: bleak trudge work involving long hours out in the cold. She absolutely loathed that, especially in the long, dark nights of winter.

Arne, his grey hair and beard more unruly than usual, continued speaking while steel-eyeing her entrance. "...Bruising around Anneka's neck suggests she was strangled in the warmth, which means indoors, but we're still awaiting the autopsy report to confirm this. Nobody goes round naked in these freezing temperatures, so her body must have been dumped. We need to find out when, and work back from there. As you know, the CCTVs around this estate have been vandalised, so we need eyewitness accounts."

"They'd have needed a car or a van. Wouldn't that have made a noise?" Jessika's eager voice interrupted from somewhere in front.

The chief glowered in her direction. "Give the girl a star. But even on a rundown estate like that, people would be asleep. Or drunk. Or high on drugs." He looked round the room. "Any other questions?"

Soldis, like everyone else, was not in a hurry to act as a lightning rod for his curmudgeonly temper, and stayed silent.

"Good." He fingered a cigarette packet on the table he leant on. "SvePol is running this enquiry live through your phones from Stockholm Central. They're analysing what CCTV footage they can get their hands on, so check regularly for an info update and change in orders. You've each been allocated one of these blocks. Now go. Before people forget."

Quiet footsteps and murmurings reinforced the movement-of-people pressure to leave the room. Soldis headed out.

"Soldis," Arne yelled. "Stay. I've got a special job for you."

She caught the edge of the door and twisted round to flatten herself against the wall. Others, with sympathetic eyes, streamed past as the room emptied. When only stragglers were rushing to escape, she made her way over to Arne.

He pulled a cigarette from his pack and fumbled in his pocket. "This needs your special touch of breaking bad news gently."

She eyed the cigarette. "That's illegal in the workplace."

"You don't have my damned sister, Brigitte, to deal with. She's flying up, by the way. SvePol ordered her to lead this case. Local knowledge baloney and all that." He pulled out a lighter, lit his cigarette and took in a lungful of smoke. "God, I needed this." The door closed, leaving them alone in the room. "You've pulled the short straw to tell the victim's boyfriend, Torsten Lindberg."

She took a few seconds to absorb this. "*The* Torsten

Lindberg, the mad millionaire recluse who lives in that crazy house made out of ice?"

"Yep. He insists you be there by eight forty-five." He blew out smoke to the side of them. "We've delayed telling the press it's Anneka on the grounds we've yet to inform the family, so Lindberg won't know she's dead. Find out what you can before you break the news."

"Then why is he expecting me?"

"He reported her missing late last night. Saw her last yesterday at eight when she went to her hairdresser."

"Anything else I should know?" This came out more as a growl of annoyance than Soldis had intended.

"You know as much as I do."

"You want me to go on to her parents afterwards?"

"No, that's my job. Unfortunately." He inhaled from his cigarette.

The smoke was making her throat sore. She pressed her lips together to prevent her from saying anything she would regret, and rushed out of the room.

#

While the uniform's newly developed flexible thermal material kept Soldis' body warm, her face was open to the freezing air. It made her think she was cold, even though she knew otherwise. The blueness of the house's sheer ice walls in the harsh white streetlights added to her chilliness, but what really gave her the shivers were the black-as-villain's-shades smooth windows, three to either side of the double door and seven along the first floor. Weird did not even start to describe it, but the sooner she got out of the cold, the better.

She rang the doorbell, held her hands around her mouth and nose, and blew out her breath to get her face warmer.

One door cracked open. A well-built man in his early thirties, dressed in sweater and ski-pants, filled the opening like he knew wearing doorframes snugly was in fashion this winter. His short blond hair was immaculately combed, and his blue eyes outshone his clean-shaven face. His lack of expression sent another shiver through her body.

She pulled out her phone, turned it face up and hit the blue "I" button. A holograph of her official ID flared into existence above the screen. "Police Officer Soldis Andersson. You asked for one of us to come round."

"Ah." He frowned and paused. "I was expecting someone... more senior."

"Our resources have been stretched with an urgent matter this morning." She kicked off the snow from her boots. "May we talk indoors?"

"Yeah, I'll suppose you'll have to do." He moved to one side to let her into the vestibule.

It took her a moment to realise the pink gleam from the walls, ceiling and floor looked as if they, too, were made of ice, yet she felt her face warming up. "That's a good imitation of ice," she said, taking off her outdoor jacket.

"The ice is real."

She stopped halfway in removing her boot. "Why isn't it melting in this warmth?"

"Very observant." Torsten smiled.

She waited for an explanation.

"Water is a very complex liquid. In fact, it's two basic liquids mixed together. You can do many things with it. Freezing it in a particular way produces this ice."

She pulled her boot fully off and tentatively placed her stockinged foot on the floor. It was much like marble, cool but not unbearably so. She frowned: her belief in millionaires leaving details to others had just taken a knock. "Interesting," she mumbled to herself, wondering whether there were other surprises in this house. She hurriedly discarded the rest of her outdoor clothes.

"This way." He led her into a large living room.

She carefully walked across some thick rugs to avoid contact with the bare ice floor. The room was so neat that the manicured plants had to be expensive imitations. The windows were hidden behind thick, red, floor-length curtains that reflected and amplified the glow from any bare ice. Even the seven-seat cream sofa – curved into the corner round a coffee table – where, with a hand gesture, he invited her to sit, had acquired a rose tinge.

Torsten glanced at his watch. "Enough time to make some coffee. Want some?"

Soldis sat down. "Please."

He stepped behind a grille of floor-to-ceiling, two-centimetre-thick ice poles, to become a moving silhouette.

Etiquette, and needing to be sensitive to a man about to learn his girlfriend had been murdered, required her to stay where she was. So she waited, trying to work out how best to question and then break the news to him.

The aroma of coffee with a hint of cinnamon hit her nose. She squinted through the slits between the poles: beyond him were a chest-high oven, a hooked-over tap and a walk-in fridge. That alcove was a kitchen, far smaller than she had expected for this size of house. It made her wonder what some of the other rooms in the house were used for: maybe a gym, an old-fashioned library, a hobby room for something like a model railway layout, or just for storage of all the stuff he might have collected during and since childhood.

Torsten emerged from the kitchenette, carrying a tray with steaming mugs and cinnamon buns, sat down, passed over her coffee and offered her the plate of buns. "Please, take one while they're warm."

His actions betrayed no worry about Anneka, as if he was in his own comfort-bubble. This was going to be an awkward interview. She picked up a bun in a serviette and took a bite. They were homemade, none of the usual traces of preserving chemicals: heavenly. "This is delicious, thank you, but do you mind if we get down to why you called for us?" She placed her phone on the table's corner, set it up for recording and only needed to hit the "R" button. "Do I have your permission to log our conversation on this phone, a copy of which will be automatically transmitted back to our police station?"

Torsten ignored it and her, and pushed a control built into

the sofa's armrest. A pair of curtains swished aside to reveal dawn breaking.

"Huh?" Dawn was not due for another couple of hours.

"Please wait and watch." He leaned forward to concentrate on the window.

"But—"

"Sh. Watch."

Soldis decided to mollify him: it would get her job done quicker in the long run. The coffee and bun were too inviting to ignore, so she sat back without hitting the "R" button to start recording, and did her best to relax.

The blue of the polar twilight lightened and the sky added more red to a dawn that could not be happening. The street outside, with its snow-covered birch and pine forest opposite, remained still for too long, enough time to let her frustration build almost to the breaking point. A female walked up and crossed the road towards them. As she came closer, what could be seen of her face beneath the hat and behind the scarf became clearer. Anneka.

Soldis half-choked on her coffee. "What the hell?"

"Watch. I'll explain later."

Soldis felt queasy, yet could not help but be fascinated by the horror of seeing a ghost. Or was it a silly rich boy's prank? "Hold it. Where's this video come from?"

"It'll be over in a few more minutes, and then we can talk."

A driverless upmarket metallic osmium grey XC30E Volvo, plate number KTA 589, stopped just ahead of Anneka. Two men wrapped in winter hats and jackets got out of the back and blocked her path. These might be the men who had killed her. Soldis felt her sickness rise even more.

Anneka nodded and obviously talked with the men, though Soldis could not, frustratingly, lip-read the words. One man pointed up the road. Anneka glanced in that direction and then at the icehouse, nodded and climbed into the car. The men turned. Soldis recognised the crooked nose of one of them. She had broken it when she'd fought the school bully, Bengt Zorn. The other man, judging by what she could see of his face, was probably a close relative.

37

The car drove away, leaving her staring at an empty street.

"That's it." Torsten drank the last of his coffee.

The broken silence stirred Soldis' mind into reacting. She had loads of questions, but ones about Anneka were the most urgent. "What bothered you about that scene? Why bring the police here to show it to us?"

"That," he said, pointing to the empty street, "happened at eleven yesterday. I've not seen or heard from Anneka since then. She's not answering her mobile or e-mails. It's not like her. Something's very wrong."

The timestamp of that video could easily be checked in so many ways once it was taken into evidence, which Soldis would arrange in due course. Torn between finding out more background information and telling Torsten about Anneka, Soldis opted to follow her instinct. "Was she worried about anything prior to that?"

He shook his head. "Just the usual."

"Which is?"

He stared at his mug. "Everyone, including her parents, think we live together as a couple. We don't. We just pretend to. In my case, it's to help stop women throwing themselves at me.... I'm a highly eligible bachelor. In her case, well, she needed to get away from the possessive boyfriend she picked up in Lund and the professors taking advantage of her postgrad work. An arrangement of mutual convenience."

She was shocked at how horrific Anneka's life had become, and knew it must have shown on her face despite her interview training. Yet this felt like not the total story and it would be better to tease out the rest rather than ask blunt questions. "I'm sorry she ended up in such a mess. She was a nice lass at school."

He looked at her closely. "Come to think of it, you do look about her age."

"Same year. We shared sports and home-keeping classes. She was the bright one. Me? I got by."

"Now I know why your name sounded so familiar. Anneka mentioned you as one of the few classmates who treated her like a person and not someone after favours: the curse of the rich kids, she calls it."

Torsten has just used the present tense: must think she is still alive. Even so, she wanted to tease out more. "I never knew that."

"I don't think you were meant to. She is desperate for genuine people." He glanced at her phone. "There's something else."

"Oh?"

"I don't want what I'm about to say to go beyond this room."

"I have to do my job."

He turned his empty mug round this way, then that, and stopped to lock eyes with her. "Only if you promise you won't let your colleagues know, unless it becomes necessary. Do I have your word?"

She was reluctant to agree, but this was clearly important to him. "How do you know that even if I make such a promise, I won't break it?"

"The very fact you're asking that question."

Her choice: getting the truth under the pretence of thinking Anneka was still alive and keeping it back from other people unless absolutely necessary; or not knowing something that might be relevant to catching the murderer. Neither made her comfortable. But there was a killer at large who had to be caught. "You have my word."

He nodded. "She's doing some research for me. On paper it's for me personally, but if successful the research can lead to a very profitable commercial product, which I would push onto the market through my private firm. My business rivals may have got wind of this and might use, let's call them *unethical* means to persuade her to talk."

"Wait. You actually work?"

He chuckled. "What did you think I do? Play around like some pampered rich boy? I tried that for a couple of weeks and got utterly bored."

He was right: she should not have typecast him. But Anneka must be the focus of her enquiries, even if this conversation was not being recorded. "How, as you put it, unethical? I mean how far would they go?"

"If they can get away without being caught, then they might go as far as kidnapping and torture. I hope not, but depends how upright the firm is. Some I wouldn't trust at all. In Stockholm, where my office is, you can get anything done if you've the right contacts in government and the police, including SvePol, so I'm told."

Soldis gulped. Although Kiruna was a town of only twenty-five thousand people, it served as the centre of Norrbotten County of three hundred thousand people, which was based heavily on mining, forestry, research at the space port, and tourism. It did not have the capacity to be a city of corruption, serious vice, industrial espionage and power struggles spilling over on every street corner. That was for the TV or cinema. "How much do your rivals know about your research?"

"Not the details, of course, but they would expect me – us – to be working on something. I'm always careful to give her only part of the problem I need solving, never the whole picture. That's what they would expect me to do, but with us living together, they might think otherwise."

"So your rivals may think she knows what your final product may be, but she doesn't?"

"That's a good summary."

This would take some explaining to Arne, and her promise to Torsten made it far more difficult. First things first. "We're going to need that video you just showed me."

"It's not a video. In fact, that was the last time we'll ever see that sequence."

"What the devil? You're worried about Anneka and yet you did not even record the evidence about your last known sighting of her?"

"No point. It won't stand up in a court of law. A good defence lawyer would slate it as fabricated artwork in the absence of detailed scientific explanation, which I'm not willing to give."

"Why?"

"It's in my interest not to."

Soldis took a few seconds to think of and reject many possible reasons why. In the end she was left with one inevitable implication that she could not reject. "You're going to tell me something I don't believe, aren't you?"

He looked at her sharply.

"Your windows? How do they do that... that delay business? And what for?"

His muscles tensed. "Very perceptive questions for an ordinary police officer."

She had been here before, with other people. Experience warned her to back off. "Sometimes I get lucky in asking the right questions. Well, no, that's not quite true either. I ask so many questions that sooner or later I am bound to hit on the one that gets an interesting reply."

"Interesting strategy." He sat back, as if weighing up his reply. "In oversimplified terms? The ice in the window has been doctored to slow down incoming light such as sunlight. In that window's case, by twenty-two hours, the longest I can manage. That window" —he pointed to the curtained one nearest the room's entrance— "by five hours and the middle one by eight hours. As to why? I have severe Seasonal Affective Disorder. You could say this is my eccentric way of dealing with the lack of light during the long hours of polar twilight."

"Why don't you move south for the winter? Someone of your wealth can surely afford it?"

"I need the Arctic cold for some of my experiments and—"

"You don't want to move your lab."

"Precisely. What's behind all these questions?"

Soldis knew the awkward moment had come. "Do you remember, when I came in, I said the police were dealing with an urgent matter?"

He nodded.

"A murder victim was found."

He gasped.

"I'm sorry to have to tell you that we believe the dead person is Anneka."

He stared into the distance for long, uncounted seconds.

"How?"

His calmness unnerved her. It suggested he had training or too much experience in coping with bad situations. "She was strangled and her naked body was dumped at the back of Bjorkplan. She was found at four-thirty this morning by a worker on their way to an early shift."

He froze like the ice around him. Even his chest stopped moving.

She touched his forearm. "Are you still with me?"

He blinked as if coming out of a trance. "They would've wanted her to talk and she didn't know everything. They'd have kept her alive for a lot longer than a day, believe me: my inventions are worth that much."

Was it his guilt of giving someone else a reason to kill Anneka talking? Or was he the murderer? Her spine chilled into an icicle. She still had to ask the standard questions. "Can you identify anyone who might want Anneka dead?"

"Her ex-boyfriend, Viggo Svensson."

"You don't happen to have his contact details?"

"I don't, but she did on her air-pad. I'll get it for you." He got up and left the room.

Soldis heard him climb the stairs and decided that as long as she could hear him rummaging around, she would stay put.

He soon returned with a rose-gold-covered tablet. "Here it is." He placed it on the table in front of her. "I'm sure your experts can crack her passwords."

"Thank you." Soldis automatically opened her evidence-gathering bag, pulled on the rubber gloves and placed the air-pad inside. She closed it, took off her gloves and thumb-printed the tab. The bag's memory-material transformed into a hard briefcase to protect its contents from accidental bumps and drops. She stood up and looked Torsten up and down. He was no different from when he had first opened the door to her, except for a hint of a few creases on his forehead. The man was cool, too cool, as if he derived some inner strength of character from some hidden force or knowledge. "You're taking all this remarkably calmly."

"I knew something was badly wrong before you came. The

most important thing now is to catch her killer. That's what I'm concentrating on, not only for her and ridding society of a criminal, but also it's in my interests."

"That's understandable. It would be helpful if you could let us have a list of those firms who'd want to steal your research, as soon as practicable. We have to follow up on all possibilities until we can discover what actually happened."

He paled, but not much. "That wouldn't be advisable."

There was that resistance again. It centred on his research and inventions. This was the first time it had come without an explanation. If he were the murderer, he would be throwing a list of them in her face to keep the police busy. Unless it was a double bluff. "Why not?"

"You would find out what I work on and how I make my money. That would not only be bad for me, but it would also end up with bad consequences for others, many others, because I could not continue my work."

"That's a rather grand claim," she snapped back.

"I'm a recluse for a good reason. I'd like it to stay that way."

Soldis realised he would not give any further answers today. Extracting those would have to be left for the formal interviews by "expert detectives". "One last question. Would you be willing to come in to formally identify the body later on today? It would save her parents doing it."

He bit his lips. "I think I can manage that."

This was the first hint of his being affected by Anneka's murder, reassuring on so many levels: from him not being a murderer and therefore not a threat to her, to his actually having some humanity. "Is there someone who you can call for company?"

"No." He paused. "I'm best left alone."

So she had been right about his experience or training. "I'd better get this back to the analysts," she said, picking up her evidence bag and standing up. "I hope we'll meet again under less stressful circumstances."

He stood. "I hope so too."

It was her dismissal. Soldis strode for the door, but slipped on a patch of uncovered floor ice. She grabbed at a shelf lined with potted plants to steady herself. Her ankle bent under her, and she screamed as pain seared through her leg; she collapsed to the floor, pulling a couple of plants down behind her.

With Torsten's help she managed to sit up, and pulled her sock off. Her ankle was red and hot. She turned her leg so the hottest part was on the ice floor. The cooling gave her some relief.

"Let me have a look," he said, staying crouched beside her foot.

"You a doctor on top of everything else?" Nevertheless, she carefully rolled her leg round to let him see the damage.

"I am what I am and do what I can." He gently touched round the edges of her ankle. "Don't think it's broken, but it's a very bad sprain." He rolled her leg back to let the ice numb her pain, and looked at her with pursed lips. "Your police chief will want you at work, won't he?"

The last question Soldis had expected. She had to let this play out. "Absolutely."

"Okay." He disappeared into the hallway and quickly returned, waving an elasticated sock in front of him. "This should keep you on your feet for at least fifteen hours."

"How?" A couple of tears slipped out of her eyes.

"It's a medical compress for ankles." He slipped it over her injured ankle and made sure it was secured snugly. "It'll take about twenty minutes for the pain to disappear. Do you want a cup of tea while you wait?"

She glanced at the broken plant-pots. "Sorry for the mess."

"Don't worry about it. There are more important things in life. Now, how about that tea?"

Guilt at her stupidity was sending her to a new low. "Yes, please."

He went off and made noises in the kitchen.

As she pulled her own sock back on, Soldis had a closer look at the compress. Its grey elastic material looked similar to Medice compresses used in hospital dramas on the TV, only smoother and snazzier. She also felt a tingling, more like a gentle sucking of stuff out of her skin; at the same time, the compress still felt tight around her ankle. The contradictory sensations were both confusing and fascinating.

The smell of camomile tea got stronger, and soft footfalls closer.

"Here, drink this." Torsten held the mug in front of her.

She looked at him. "You're the man that invented the Medice compress, aren't you?"

"How did you come up with that crazy idea?"

"Because that" —she pointed at the one on her foot— "is non-standard, probably an experimental improvement."

He glanced at her foot. "Yes, you're right. An ordinary police officer would not have picked up on that. Are you a special police officer of some sort?"

Soldis chuckled. "What, here in Kiruna? There are too few people to warrant that kind of thing."

"So I thought." He paused. "Can I ask a favour? Well, two, actually."

"Depends what they are."

"The first is let me know when that compress wears out its usefulness. You'll know, believe me."

"That's the least I can do. And the second?"

"Don't tell your colleagues I'm the genius and owner of the company that makes Medice compresses. I'd rather stay out of the limelight."

"Did Anneka know?"

"She was helping me improve them."

She wanted to agree, because he had shown her kindness in the face of her idiocy, but she had responsibilities. "I won't unless it becomes relevant to solving Anneka's murder. Then I'll have no choice."

"Fair enough. Now let's get you more comfortable while that compress does its work." He took the mug off her to place it on the shelf, and helped her up and back to the sofa.

As if by mutual agreement, they talked about anything except Anneka's murder or Soldis' being a failure of a police officer. Half an hour later she walked out of the room without the slightest twinge of pain.

#

When Soldis entered the operations room, the allocation map was up on the screen. Each block had been partially coloured in translucent red to denote the proportion of those who had not answered their doors, and a smaller segment of green for completed interviews. The box in the top right-hand corner showed a time window from ten thirty the previous evening to four thirty in the morning for the dumping of Anneka's body. Hardly any progress had been made.

Arne, presumably returned from seeing Anneka's parents, was talking to a smartly dressed woman who looked very like him.

"There you are at last," Arne said on noticing her.

"I had to drop off Anneka's air-pad into Evidence so they can dig out the contact details of her ex-boyfriend, Viggo Svensson. He's the possessive type and therefore a possible suspect. It'll also give us all her internet correspondence."

"The boyfriend accusation is based on what?" the woman asked.

"Torsten Lindberg's statement."

"Her current boyfriend," Arne added.

Soldis decided not to contradict him.

"He's already on our suspect list," Arne added.

"I got the impression Torsten had more to gain with her alive than dead." Soldis tried to keep her voice as matter-of-fact as possible.

"You may be right," the woman said. "I need to listen to the recording of his witness statement. I presume you've logged that into Evidence as well."

"He didn't give permission."

The woman raised her right eyebrow. "He's hiding something."

"Give him a break. He's just been told about Anneka's death," Arne put in.

"Even so, I'll have to interview him myself now." She headed out of the room, forcing Soldis to step out of her way.

Once the door closed behind the woman, Soldis let out a whistle. "That your sister, Brigitte?"

"Who got out the wrong side of bed this morning," the chief replied. "There's no need to be diplomatic about her. I know what a pain she is."

She suppressed a snigger. "What's Bengt Zorn up to these days?"

Arne's blue eyes narrowed so much they became lasers. "He's a bouncer at that lovely den of crime and vice, the Iron Fist club."

She hated her chief when he was in his dry-sense-of-humour mood. If there were a national competition in portraying this Swedish trait, he would win hands down. "Nothing's changed then, and little Jonni Rasmussen is still calling the shots."

Arne shook his head. "He's just the owner. Latest rumour has it there's someone else behind him. With bigger clout."

This was news to Soldis, but it fitted in with Bengt using an expensive Volvo. "A big name in business, I bet."

The chief cocked his head to one side. "What do you know that I don't?"

Soldis felt her face warm at letting a semi-detail slip after having promised Torsten she would not say anything. "Something that won't stand up in court for now."

"So Lindberg did talk."

Soldis nodded, then sniggered. "Your sister will meet her match."

"I hope he won't complain."

"I doubt it."

"Good. She needs taking down a peg or two. What else did he tell you?"

Caught between her duty and her principles to keep her promise, she struggled within herself. "Anneka was seen getting into an expensive car with Bengt at about eleven yesterday morning."

"Hellfire. If that mob has upped its game to murder... Did you get the registration of the car?"

"Yes."

"And?"

"Look, I can't see Bengt ever doing something like that."

"How would you know?"

"Bengt and I were in the same class at school. He had criminal tendencies for sure, but not the cold heart of a killer. He wouldn't even shoot elk when his father tried to teach him to hunt."

"He could have changed. Desperation can do strange things to people."

"True, but..."

"You're not convinced, are you?"

Soldis shook her head. "Let me talk to him at the club tonight. He's more likely to give me answers than if you bring him in for questioning."

The chief stared at her for a few seconds in a concentrated thinking mode. "Registration number?"

"Chief!"

"I need to check any story he comes up with."

She really had no choice if she wanted to keep this job. "KTA 589."

"If what you find out from him corroborates what the vehicle tracking department comes up with, and he just dropped her off somewhere nothing to do with this case, that'll avoid me ruffling their feathers." The chief sat and put his head in his hands. "This is going to get very messy," he mumbled. "And one other thing, make sure my sister doesn't hear about it. She'll go in all guns blazing and we'll get nowhere."

"On it, Chief." She looked at the map. "Which is my door-knocking section?"

#

Soldis swapped her outdoor clothes for a ticket from the Iron Fist's cloakroom attendant. Her swimsuit spangles outfit, as she had nicknamed it, was a little tight on her due to Christmas overeating. Every time the disco's door opened, a catchy tune or weird noise blared out, accompanied by the beat of stomping feet of the

Viking-rockers.

Only the dance floor's entrance was free of muscled guards. The other three doors, stairway and lifts had them either side. A scar on one of their hands caught her attention. It edged a patch of skin that was too smooth compared with the rest, and far smoother than any skin-graft pictures she had seen in the social media. Jonni obviously spared no expense on his loyal people, using such plush synth-skin. Repairs were legal; cosmetic surgery to replace old or ugly skin was illegal because of health risks.

Rumours were Jonni had such multi-coloured synth-skin escorts. She shuddered at the horror of the grotesque thought.

She could not see Bengt anywhere.

"That ticket only allows you in the disco and bar," the attendant said. "If you want other services, like the casino, pole-dancing entertainment or smoke room, it'll be extra."

"No, I was only looking for an old school-friend who works here, Bengt Zorn. No matter. I'll catch up with him another time."

"I'll let him know you asked after him, Ms...?"

"Soldis." She slipped her ticket into the small shoulder bag.

"And the surname?" The attendant smiled, eying her costume appreciatively.

She smiled back. "I'm the one who broke his nose."

A flash of utter surprise crossed his face before he straightened up. "I'll let him know you're here."

"I'll be at the bar." She headed into the disco. The "Oarsmen" hit was playing. Men on the dance floor cavorted a physical workout, while women stood around the edge swaying to the music's rhythm. Soldis meandered her way through to the bar, sat on an empty stool and ordered single malt whisky.

"May I suggest the Talisker, peated and smoky over fruity flavours? Something you can really savour."

"I'll try it. How much?"

"For you, my dear, on the house."

"Thank you." Her message had got through. All she had to do was sit and wait.

Half an hour and a music-induced splitting headache later, Bengt sat down beside her with the tie undone in his otherwise immaculate black bouncer uniform.

"Dancing would stop the headache."

"That obvious, is it?"

"Yes. What brings you here?" He snapped his fingers and ordered two more whiskies.

"A hell of a day at work. I take it you've heard the news."

"Yep." The drinks arrived. "Let's drink to Anneka."

As one they picked up their glasses, clinked them together and said: "To Anneka." Their glasses hit the bar as one.

"You've a good taste in whisky," Bengt said.

Soldis smiled. "Your bartender does."

"Ah, he is a good man." He paused. "What really brings you here?"

"Where did you take Anneka yesterday morning?"

"What're you talking about?" The tell-tale twitch in his left eye gave away he was nervous.

"Let me refresh your memory: KTA 589, Volvo."

He opened his mouth and closed it.

"You don't have to tell me anything. But it would help if you could say where you left her. That way" —she glanced meaningfully round the room— "SvePol won't need to take too much interest in this place."

He frowned. "Why the favour?"

"No favour. I want to find Anneka's murderer and get SvePol the hell out of Kiruna. Me? I like the quiet life."

"I see." He was still holding his glass, until he finally squeezed it so hard that it cracked halfway down the side. "She was one of the few classmates who didn't try to use me."

"Meaning I did?"

"No. You were straight with me." He rubbed his nose. "I want you to catch the son of a bitch who killed her," he growled.

"Then help us."

"I had nothing to do with her murder. Honest," he said, desperate, pleading.

"I believe you. Where did you take her?"

"Jonni asked me to take her to Esrange as a favour for someone. He didn't say who. We dropped her off at the bio-lab at the west end of the range in time for a late lunch."

"Any idea who she met?"

"No. We had to be somewhere else."

Soldis filled in the blanks herself. Esrange was an international rocket range forty kilometres east of Kiruna, which attracted people from all over the world, some of them running illicit goods for a bit of extra cash. Bengt was there to pick them up. Equally, the new bio-lab would be small, have very few people going in and out, and be a good place for a meeting on the quiet.

"What did you say to Anneka to persuade her to come with you?"

His eyes widened. "You have a witness to our picking her up?"

She put on the sweetest, most sarcastic smile she could muster in spite of her headache.

"You're not going to answer that," Bengt said. "All I said was that David had found something of interest to her and wanted to urgently meet her."

"David who?"

"I don't know."

Anneka must have known who she would be meeting. "Did you tell her you worked for Jonni?"

Understanding flickered across his face. "Yes."

"So Anneka and Jonni must have been in touch about arranging a meet with this David," she said, more to herself than him.

"Sounds like it."

"Is there any chance you could find his surname? Give us something to go on."

"You're asking a lot."

"If your people have nothing to do with this, it would help get SvePol out of Kiruna sooner."

"I'll ask. No guarantees. But it'll have to be an anonymous tip."

"Understood."

"To your personal number. Not your work phone."

She pulled out her pencil phone, hit the "on" switch at one

end. A holograph rose with all the control tabs showing. "Here." she presented it to him.

Bengt went through the standard method of phoning and capturing the number, and then smiled. "Want another?" He held up his empty glass.

Business done, she relaxed, but her headache had noticeably worsened. She stroked her head as if to push it away, but it stubbornly remained. "If you don't mind, I've got a busy day tomorrow."

#

The operations room was packed for the progress briefing at six the following morning. Soldis stood at the back, stifling a yawn.

Brigitte strutted up and down in front of the map. "Anneka left her hairdresser shortly after ten thirty to return to the icehouse. Her last sighting on town CCTVs was at Ostgatan, within three hundred metres of her home and heading in that direction. Torsten Lindberg maintains she never entered the house, but she could have come and gone without his noticing. We need to find out what she did for the rest of the day."

Soldis opened her mouth to speak, and Jessika piped up. "Do we have time of death yet?"

"All they can say for certain is after ten thirty in the evening, but could be as late as three in the morning. It depends how long her body was out in the cold. So we need her movements until three in the morning. SvePol will direct your enquiries while they analyse more CCTV footage."

"What about her phone records?" Jessika continued. "Do they give a clue to meeting someone?"

"No."

Soldis was stunned. The geeks would have analysed her air-pad for contacts and plans by now. Unless Anneka had access to a third phone or other communication device, Brigitte would know about Jonni putting her in touch with "David". Soldis' ankle itched in sympathy with her mental prickliness that something was off with the domineering woman.

"And before you ask," Brigitte continued, "she didn't talk to anyone in the CCTV footage we do have. You," she said, pointing in Soldis' direction. "What were you about to say?"

"Sounds like she took a taxi or private car to me."

Jessika jumped up. "She could have walked into a house where there's no CCTV coverage."

"SvePol is examining both possibilities. Until we find which is correct, we'll work both."

A universal grumble echoed round the room.

"Yes, that means more door-to-door, first concentrating around the stretch between her last sighting and the icehouse, and taking note of any passing cars. You'll—"

Soldis' private phone vibrated. She dug it out of her jacket pocket and checked who the call was from: Bengt.

"—have your instructions on your phones. As usual, keep checking them for updates and remember it's as important to know where she has not been as where she—"

Soldis slipped from the room and opened the message: "David Jackson, specialist in lichens." Her ankle's itch became an ache. Time to make a call.

Torsten's irritable face filled the risen holograph. "Is this business or pleasure?"

"Neither. My ankle has just started to make itself felt."

He broke out into a smile. "Thank you. I reckon you have an hour before it becomes too painful to walk on. Can you make it to my place by then?"

"Why?"

"I have a new experiment for you to try."

"I'm on my way." She hastily closed down her phone as people started filing out of the room, and brought out her official phone to check for instructions.

The chief, one of the first to leave the room, eyed her. "Walk with me." He grabbed her elbow and steered her down the corridor until they reached his office. He pushed her inside and closed the door behind them. "What's going on?"

"I've had an unofficial tip-off."

"How unofficial?"

"Very."

"Anything to do with our conversation yesterday?"

"Yes."

"I see. What was the tip?"

"Anneka got a lift out to the new bio-lab at Esrange and arrived there about one-thirty to meet an expert in lichens, David Jackson."

The chief frowned as he fumbled in his pocket and took out a pack of cigarettes. "What's their relationship?"

"I don't know."

He took out a cigarette. "Hm. This case has just gone beyond weird." He pulled out a lighter from a different pocket.

The ache in her ankle was getting stronger. "Look, Chief, I don't have time right now. I need to get to the icehouse."

"Why?"

She grimaced, wondering whether or not to tell him about the compress.

"I know that look, and out-stubborning a cat is far easier than a Swede on a mission," the chief continued. "This is the deal. I drive you there, wait outside while you do whatever you have to do and drive you back. In return, on the way back you tell me what's going on, 'unofficially'. Then I'll know what to do if you get in trouble."

Soldis was out of the room. "Let's move. I'm on the clock."

#

By the time Soldis left the chief outside in the car and stumbled through the icehouse's open door, her ankle was all agony. Torsten helped her to the sofa, quickly swapped the compress for a new one, which felt even smoother, was flesh-coloured and seemed to fit her ankle much better than the old one. He fetched the chief in and served up coffee.

Arne immediately noticed and stared at Soldis' ankle. "I hope you're not after a desk job, because we need people walking the streets."

"Give me a little while and I'll be fine," she said through

gritted teeth.

"Really?"

"Absolutely," Torsten said. "Shouldn't take more than a quarter of an hour."

It took only ten minutes before the pain subsided and Soldis, although shaken, felt more her normal self, staring at an empty mug.

"Torsten," she finally said, "did Anneka have a second phone or a second computer?"

"Yes. Wait here." Torsten left and returned a few minutes later waving an older air-pad version. "Anneka used this as her backup computer for important data she was happy for me to see." He sat and opened her account with the screen facing them all.

"How did you get in?" the chief asked.

Torsten gave him a quizzical look. "Anneka gave me her password, of course."

"Just checking," the chief said.

They all watched the screen as Torsten switched its Wi-Fi off. "This should leave her e-mails as she last saw it." He opened her mail app. "Looks like the last time she used this was six months ago."

"And she only has the one address," the chief added. "Any other phones?"

"Not that I know of," Torsten replied.

"Could she have used yours?"

"Mine are all thumbprint-locked or need voice recognition."

"Wait," Soldis said. "Did she have a phone on her?"

Torsten grimaced. "Probably, but it was a special one with a deactivated GPS. No way of finding it unless she had it switched on, which she normally didn't."

SvePol would have automatically checked that. This line of questioning had come to a natural end. That left her other topic. "Did Anneka's work involve lichens?"

Torsten glanced over to the chief. "Short answer is no. Long answer is it was her postgrad work trying to develop bioluminescent lichen that made me contact her in the first place.

I was searching for a cure to my Seasonal Affective Disorder and I thought – as it turned out, incorrectly – that bioluminescence might help. The rest as they say is history. Why?"

"Did she ever talk about a David Jackson in connection with lichens?"

"I think they used to work together in Lund. She would probably have kept track of his work since she moved up here. Where're these questions heading?"

"Would there be any reason why she would want to meet him?"

Torsten stared at her for a few seconds, then connected Anneka's tablet to the Wi-Fi.

"What the devil?" the chief muttered.

"I need to check a few things," Torsten replied as he did searches using words that had no meaning to Soldis. And flash-read the results.

Five minutes and umpteen screen-views later, Torsten banged his fist on the table and shoved the air-pad away from him. He sat back with his arms folded, staring into nowhere.

The calmness of the ice man had broken. Soldis guessed why. "What's wrong?" She was giving Torsten a chance to explain to the chief.

"Dr Jackson was looking into an area close to Anneka's current focus of her scientific research."

"Since when did a rich playboy kid do techno mumbo-jumbo?" the chief asked.

Torsten paused. "Anneka explained some of these things to me."

Soldis sensed Torsten had retreated into his shell of secrecy, and had to say something to get things moving again. "We think Anneka met Jackson at lunchtime the day before yesterday at Esrange."

The chief whipped his phone out and hit the call tab to Kiruna police station's coordinating unit.

"Chief," Leif said from the phone's screen, "what do you need?"

"The whereabouts of a Dr David Jackson, research scientist

in lichens, used to work in Lund. I need the info like yesterday."

Leif was already tapping away when he said, "On it, Boss. Will get back to you as soon as I know anything." The screen blanked.

The chief looked from Torsten to Soldis and back again. "Whatever's going on between you two, sort it," he growled. "Why her interest in lichens *now*? I want the no-beating-about-the-bush answer."

Soldis cringed against her seat.

"She was working to improve the Medice compresses," Torsten replied. "As you can appreciate, big businesses and rival firms would have an interest in getting their hands on that research."

"Why here in Kiruna?"

"Apart from getting away from her vicious ex-boyfriend, you mean?" Torsten glared back.

"Yes."

"She used to collect local lichen samples. Said something about their variability helped speed up her research."

The chief's phone rang. He tapped it to accept the call.

Leif's face appeared on the screen. "Chief, Jackson is staying at the Scandic Ferrum hotel. Booked in there three days ago and hasn't booked out since."

"Hellfire," the chief said. "Find him. Mark it top priority."

"Will do, but you'll have to okay it with your sister."

"What do you mean?"

"She went ballistic when I told her about your search request. Muttered something about wasting time."

"It isn't. Now get to it." He switched the phone off before Leif had a chance to argue, and stood up. "Torsten, pull together a description of what Anneka was doing in her research in terms that even the stupidest police officer can understand."

"She may not have told me everything."

"Do the best you can."

"You," he said, nodding towards Soldis, "with me."

#

57

The reception desk in the Scandic Ferrum was the standard "book yourself in and out" type, but as this was a high-end hotel, next to it was a female receptionist wearing a dated dark blue jacket and white blouse, behind an old-fashioned desk. She smiled at the chief and Soldis, her teeth brilliantly white against her deep faux tan. "How may I help the police?"

"We would like to talk to Dr David Jackson, please," the chief replied. "Is he in?"

The receptionist tapped and checked her screen. "Yes. Do you wish me to ask him to come down?"

"Please."

She rang through and waited for a reply, her smile slowly dying. She finally put the phone down. "I'm sorry. Although he's registered as still in the room, he didn't answer."

Soldis glanced down at her ankle and its compress, a corporate secret that spelt massive profits for whoever got it to the patent rights first. And Anneka had been working to improve it "First Anneka, and now Jackson..." she hinted at the chief.

The receptionist caught her breath sharply. "Do you mean the woman who's been killed?"

"Yes," the chief replied. "We think Dr Jackson could help us with our enquiries."

Soldis could not blame the chief for following procedure. "Dr Jackson could have been working with Anneka. He could be next on the killer's hit list."

"Is that a real possibility?" the receptionist asked.

"Yes," Soldis replied immediately.

The receptionist snatched a key-card from behind the desk. "Come with me." She rushed across the foyer, ran up two flights of stairs and along a corridor past room doors facing each other, until she reached the last on her right.

The chief and Soldis pulled out their guns, their fingerprints unlocking the safety catches. She snatched the key-card from the receptionist and used it. The door lock's green light came on. She pushed the door open and twisted round to stand with her back to the wall.

No sound other than the whirr of air conditioning.

Soldis moved first into the room's hallway. She checked the bathroom, as the door was open. Nothing odd there. She moved on into the bedroom proper. Jackson lay splayed on the bed with a gunshot hole in his chest. She checked under the bed and in the cupboards for anyone hiding there.

The chief followed her in to take Jackson's pulse. He shook his head.

Holstering her gun, she noticed the skin did not have a waxy appearance. Jackson had been killed in the last hour or so. "Damn it, we were just too late."

The chief pulled out his phone. "Brigitte's going to have a field day."

Soldis glanced at the empty desk and the opened empty safe in the cupboard. She rapidly searched the room's drawers, his suitcase and briefcase, and very gingerly felt his pockets. "There's no tablet or smartphone. The killer must have taken them."

"Why the interest in his gadgets?"

"Whoever killed him has probably now got access to his research."

"The gadgets are traceable."

"They'll copy the data and ditch the tablets and smartphones."

"You're right, again." The chief pulled out his phone and hit the red tab for an emergency assist from the coordinating unit.

"What is it, Chief?" Leif said.

"We've discovered a second murder victim in room 228 at the Scandic Ferrum. Send the usual first-response team."

"On it, Chief."

He snapped his phone shut and turned to Soldis. "Get to the icehouse pronto. Drag Lindberg into protective custody. He's probably next on our killer's list. Hurry."

#

Soldis skidded round the final blind bend in the lamp-lit polar twilight. A glimpse of the icehouse's door with an oval-shaped hole in it confirmed her worst fears: the killer had already arrived.

She hit two buttons on her dashboard, to open a call to the coordination centre and to request emergency assistance.

"What is it, Soldis?" Leif asked.

"Break-in at the icehouse. Possible murder in progress."

She crashed her car into the door and was pushed forward against her seatbelt. The would-be killer or killers would be distracted enough by the noise to slow them down.

After being slammed back into her seat, Soldis jumped out of the car, pulled out her gun from its holster, and the ID pad in her glove transferred her fingerprint to release the safety catch. She raced, crouched below the front windows; rounded the side of the house, flattened herself against the back wall and let her eyes adjust to twilight with only snow-reflected lamplight.

Black windows were above. Steps led down from the door onto flat snow, probably covering a lawn, which was surrounded by snow-laden birches and pines. It was eerily still, no wind. There were no footmarks in the snow, so if Torsten was still alive, he either had escaped through the front door onto trodden ice or was still in the house.

Soldis glanced back round the corner: as expected, her footmarks were visible in the snow. She had to move fast. She ran along the back of the house, over the steps. To draw the killers her way, she shot at the thick door to gain their attention. She dashed out into the nearest part of the forest to hide behind a very old birch tree, leaving a trail of footprints for them to follow.

She slid down to sit with her back to the tree and the house, made compacted snowballs and waited.

After an eternity, she heard snow being crunched: sounded like two people walking towards her.

She grabbed one snowball and threw it towards the tailgate of her car, which she could see just beyond the corner of the house, in the hope it would make sufficient noise to make them at least hesitate, if not divert them completely.

One set of crunches sped up; the other set was noticeable by its silence. Damn. They had sussed her tactic. She had better move, and keep moving. Her nose caught a whiff of burning wood.

Soldis threw two snowballs high up and deeper into the forest to shake the snow down from some of the pines and distract the killer still behind her, got up and threw two more towards the car. A creak from above made her look up. Snow was dropping from a large branch that was bending down and about to break off and drop too close to her.

Soldis ran diagonally away from the icehouse, towards the road, to hide under the low branches of a pine. She skirted the tree trunk and took aim at the man running towards where her last snowball had landed: Jonni Rasmussen, holding a gun.

She shot at his legs. He limped and then dropped to the ground holding his bloodied left leg with one hand and shooting in her direction with the other. Pain seared through her right shoulder as she ducked back under the pine. She had been shot.

Blood drops stained the snow by Soldis' feet. She rubbed her hand over where she had been hit, and saw her glove was smeared with blood. She pulled out a hankie and pressed it against the wound.

"Keep shooting, Jonni," a familiar female voice shouted.

It was so out of place that it took Soldis a full three everlasting seconds to recognise it belonged to the chief's sister.

And another three to realise she had missed too many coincidences that pointed to her involvement. The last was the timing of Dr Jackson's murder: just after Brigitte must have heard the chief was searching for him.

Her shoulder started to numb. The adrenaline override was kicking in. All Soldis could do was play for time and hope her colleagues got here before Brigitte and Jonni killed her. "Tell me something," she shouted at Brigitte. "What did Lindberg have that you wanted? He never told me." She desperately looked round for the best possible escape. None of her options looked any good.

"Waiting for your colleagues to turn up, are we? Well, I've called them off." Her crunching footsteps came closer. "Bet you didn't know he's the inventor of the Medice compress? Earned millions from it."

"So what?" Soldis placed her hand high on a low branch to reduce the blood flow to that arm and its wounded shoulder.

The footsteps paused. "He's invented a new one, lasts longer and heals quicker. But those aren't its most important properties. It's got strength, elasticity and smoothness: synth-skin you could die for. But can we find his latest invention anywhere in the lab? He's hidden it somewhere. You wouldn't happen to know where?"

She knew exactly where. It was around her ankle. In the distance, police car sirens blared, probably on their way to the Scandic Ferrum. "How would I? He was secretive enough as it was." A thought occurred to her: they would not have killed Torsten until they had his secret compress. "You can ask Torsten."

"He's not being very forthcoming."

The use of the present tense confirmed he was still alive. "That's a shame."

"You sound as if you already knew about the new compress."

She saw her opportunity to stay alive long enough for the chief to find her. "Only what Torsten told me, not that I understood half of the geek-talk."

"Ah." The footsteps started scrunching closer again. "I know how to burn where it really hurts."

"Burn?"

"Oh yes. You wouldn't think this little laser Lindberg uses in his lab for precision work had such power, would you? He gets away with it because the beam is so narrow."

There was that burning wood smell again, but this time with a hint of pine. Dollops of snow dropped beside her. Above her, a branch about a third of the way up the tree had bent down. She could just make out a white glow close to where the branch was partly broken. She blinked hard, disbelieving. Portable lasers with that amount of power were gizmos used in science fiction, not in the real world of the here-and-now.

Soldis stared back down at the blood-drenched snow: an idea so crazy that it belonged in cartoon-land popped into her head. She tested the springiness of a long, low branch next to her. It might just work. It was the only idea she had. "Is that precision laser another of Torsten's inventions?" she asked, trying to buy more time. She quickly compacted some more snowballs, making sure that as much of her frozen blood as possible was in them.

Brigitte laughed as the white line jiggled around the branch. "Oh yes. A nice little bonus for us."

The damaged branch creaked above her. She placed her snowballs on the pulled-back branch and let go.

The branch sprang back into its normal position, throwing a volley in Brigitte's direction. Soldis, gun in her left hand, edged round the opposite side of the tree and knelt to point her gun at Brigitte.

Brigitte was seven metres ahead, regaining her balance and bringing her silver laser to point at Soldis. "You bitch."

The sirens were a little louder. The police cars were coming their way after all.

"Drop that laser," Soldis said.

The laser passed over her hand holding her gun. Smoke rose from the glove, and her hand burned hot. She screamed, sank onto her knees and dropped her gun. With its fingerprint plate cracked by a laser scar, it was useless.

The laser melted a thin furrow in the snow towards Jonni and stayed on him while he writhed, until smoke rose out of his chest. He lay very still.

"You'll never get away with this," Soldis shouted through her new pain.

"Oh, yes I will." Brigitte walked over to pick up and holster Jonni's gun.

Soldis recognised it as a standard police-issue gun, and there was only one other police officer here: Brigitte. It had to be hers, with Jonni's fingerprints keyed to it. Solid evidence, if she could safeguard it.

Brigitte turned the laser toward Soldis. "Jonni here had a good reason to want you dead. You suspected him quite rightly of strangling Anneka. So he killed you, and then rather than be captured by me, committed suicide. With you dead, who is to say I'm lying? Of course, you'll get a hero's commendation." She eyed the line of sight so that it would appear to have been fired from Jonni's hand before he fell.

Soldis struggled to stand, but was feeling light-headed. She had lost too much blood.

Brigitte screamed, clutched her chest and fell slowly forward to lie still in the snow. An ice javelin, shining in the first red light of dawn, stuck up from her back.

She blinked. She had seen it before. Where? One of the poles dividing Torsten's kitchen from his lounge.

Torsten stood just outside the opened back door, in T-shirt and jogging trousers, shivering. "Is she... dead? ...I didn't mean to..."

Two police cars skidded to a stop beside the road, and the chief jumped out of one of them.

Soldis' vision dimmed into blankness.

#

At last, after all the prodding and poking, the nurses wheeled Soldis into the quiet of a private ward. She could get some much-needed sleep.

The chief walked in, more dishevelled and dark-eyed than ever. "Thank goodness. The doctors predict you'll make a good recovery."

"Only if I get some sleep."

"What the hell happened out there?"

"The only evidence you need is Brigitte's gun. It's keyed for Jonni Rasmussen's use."

The chief's jaw dropped.

"Torsten will tell you the rest," Soldis continued.

"He's not saying a damned thing. Insists he needs to give you skin grafts for your wounds. He's gone completely loopy. Since when did he become an expert in those?"

She glanced down at her bandaged hand with a small spot of red blood soaking through. Underneath was a pretty messed-up hand. Skin grafts. That was what it was all about: the illegal designer ones. The new compress was a step in the right direction, which was why Brigitte and Jonni wanted it. Jackson must have worked for them as their synth skin developer and manufacturer and, once Arne had connected him with Anneka, Brigitte had him silenced. It all fitted into place.

"You know someone must have been behind Brigitte, don't you?"

"That's SvePol's problem, now the focus has switched to Stockholm."

"Good." She closed her eyes. Those new grafts were probably another trial, but Torsten would not make the offer unless he was pretty sure he could succeed. At the same time, she felt humbled that he had singled her out for this much-needed gift. Maybe it was his way of saying thank you for saving his life. She opened her eyes. "Let Torsten do the grafts. On one condition. He gives you a statement first, in simple words, of what happened."

"But—"

She closed her eyes. "I really do need my sleep."

HOLO-SWEET

E. J. Tett

Silver stood in front of the captain's desk and wiped her clammy hands on her purple overalls as she waited for acknowledgement. The room was cool and almost spotlessly clean but for a tea-drop stain on the desk, that her janitorial expertise brought to her attention.

Captain Jamerson sat behind the desk, poring over her holoscreen – the words were visible through to the other side, so that to Silver they appeared backwards and made no sense. Probably written in alien. Silver didn't know the captain could speak alien, and she caught herself smiling at the thought of Justice Jamerson standing in front of a room full of blue-skinned other-worlders, addressing them in their own tongue. Especially as the captain was notoriously bad-tempered about aliens.

Realising she might never be noticed, Silver cleared her throat. "Ma'am?"

Justice pushed the screen aside, took one look at Silver and said, "Oh, for goodness' sake. I told them I needed a thespian. A thespian. Not a lesbian. Nobody around here listens to a damn word I say."

"Um." Silver's cheeks burned. "No, ma'am, nobody sent me here. It's about Athanasia."

The captain got to her feet and walked around her desk to stand beside the window. She looked out to the vast expanse of space, though there was nothing much to look at other than the stars. Maybe a planet or two. A few moons. "What about her?"

"She's refusing to fly to Alkeemik." She winced, expecting the captain's temper to show itself.

Instead, Justice turned and rolled her eyes. "I haven't got the time or the patience for one of her hissy fits. Tell her she will do as her captain commands." She knocked on the wall. "Hear that, old girl? You will fly to Alkeemik or I will have you sold for scrap."

Silver grinned, imagining the pretty little ship-sprite folding her arms and pouting at the insult. She waited for the captain to return to her seat before she asked, "What do you need a thespian for, Cap'n?"

"Look at this." Justice twisted the holoscreen so Silver could see, though it still looked alien to her. Justice gave an impatient tut. "It's Shakespeare, girl, Shakespeare. Please tell me you know who that is?"

Shakespeare? The name rang a bell. "Isn't he the captain of the Titania?"

"He is a sixteenth-century British playwright!" Justice's voice rose in indignation. "Goodness me, the level of education..." She trailed off, shaking her head. "I need actors so I can see for myself what one of these blasted plays is all about; they make very little sense written down like this."

"Maybe there will be actors on Alkeemik," Silver suggested. She'd have to have a word with the ship – convince her that it wouldn't be so bad to fly to the red planet.

"Maybe there will be." Justice drummed her fingers on the desk, her nails tapping the polished surface. "Was there anything else?"

"No. I'll uh... speak to Athanasia." She snapped a salute and then turned on her heel and left.

#

There was a time, shortly after she'd been promoted from her position as janitor, that Silver had thought she might get better quarters. But no. Her room was still the one next to the engine room, small and noisy and with an air vent that rattled so much she should probably look at fixing it sometime soon.

She was an advisor now. Members of the crew called her the Ship Whisperer. Ship Botherer was another one, though she didn't like the sound of that so much. And it meant she got to spend most of her time entertaining Athanasia and keeping her occupied so she didn't think about killing the crew. Again.

As jobs went, it was pretty much the best one she'd ever had. Anything that kept her from having to clear up the aftermath of a bout of space sickness was like manna from heaven. Whatever manna was. Something to do with bread?

Silver frowned as she shrugged off her purple overalls, leaving them in a pile on the floor. Janitors wore grey. Technicians blue. Advisors wore purple. Apparently. Though she'd never seen Barkley, the captain's advisor, wear any sort of overalls at all. Not that she minded wearing purple overalls. Athanasia was a big fan of the colour, telling her it brought out the green of her eyes. The ship could be such a flirt sometimes.

Anyway, she was off duty now, so she changed into jeans and a T-shirt and let her hair down from its tail, giving it a cursory brush and a quick spritz with the shine spray. She checked her appearance in the mirror and then headed out of her quarters to the room next door.

Briefly, she placed a hand on the metal casing of the ship's engine, feeling it throb. Then she approached the glass tube in the centre of the room and touched its surface. "Athanasia?"

A small ball of light appeared in the middle of the tube and then expanded to fill it before it came together again and formed into the shape of a person. A very pretty female person. A wave of affection flowed from the tube, making Silver's fingers tingle.

"I'm afraid we're going to have to go to Alkeemik."

Why?

"You know why. We need to pick up supplies."

Why?

Silver took her hand away from the glass. "Please don't start that. Look, we won't be there long. We'll take the shuttle down, stock up and then be on our merry way again. I don't know why you don't want to go there anyway."

Athanasia folded her arms and lifted her chin. *It's full of whores.*

"I doubt the *whole* planet is full of whores," Silver said. "Anyway, I'm not interested."

I saw you.

"What?"

I saw you looking.

"Looking at what?" Silver asked.

Another woman.

"The ship is full of women, of course I look at them!" Silver exclaimed. "I can't walk around with my head down, I'll have an accident. Besides, they're real women—"

I'm real.

"—with breasts I can actually get my hands on!" She realised she'd raised her hands to Athanasia's chest height on the glass, and moved them quickly to her sides. "Sorry."

I love you.

Silver sighed and sank to the floor, her back to the glass tube. "I know," she said. "And I love you. I do. I just miss being able to touch someone."

The steady thrum of the engine grew louder and Silver sat up a little straighter. She turned, only to find the glass tube was empty.

#

They were going to Alkeemik. The announcement came through shipcom when Silver tuned in. She lay on her bunk on her back, staring at the ceiling and hardly listening to the rest of the news. So Athanasia had decided after all and not bothered telling her. It unnerved her. The ship told her everything. Everything. She was the Ship Whisperer.

"Off," she said. She sighed loudly when shipcom didn't respond, and repeated, louder, "OFF." Then she smacked the wall until she had silence.

She lay for a long while, trying not to think too much but thinking the same things over and over and over. Athanasia was upset. And she'd been the one to upset her.

Eventually, she slept.

#

Silver had watched the red planet of Alkeemik grow larger and larger from the space deck. Then she'd headed back down to the engine room and tried to get Athanasia to talk to her, with no success. When the call came to board the shuttle, she waited in line with the others in the hangar and boarded behind Barkley, Justice's advisor.

"Cap'n already on board?" she asked him as she ducked her head and entered the shuttle.

"Captain Jamerson has an important meeting and has asked that I take her place instead," Barkley said. He seemed put out by this, and fussed with his belt, cursing it until Silver leaned over and connected it for him. "Thank you," he said. "I'm to speak with the Hallorn stockist and arrange transport of the goods myself. You know what these people are like, they'll only speak to ship captains half the time; I've absolutely no idea what to say to the man if he refuses our price."

Silver shrugged. It wasn't her problem. "What meeting?" she asked.

"What?"

"What's the important meeting?"

"Don't you know?"

"I wouldn't ask if I knew," she said, rolling her eyes.

"Well it seems rather odd that you don't know, given your position," Barkley said. He wiped his palms nervously on his trousers as the shuttle's engine started up. "She's talking to Athanasia."

Silver felt a twinge of something stir uneasily in her guts. Space sickness? No, she never got sick. Jealousy? She frowned. "What about?"

"How should I know?" Barkley asked impatiently.

Silver rested her head back against the restraints and glowered to herself. It was nothing to worry about. Athanasia was probably doing this to wind her up. The ship probably *wanted* to make her jealous. She realised Barkley was still speaking to her. "Hmm?"

"I said what are you doing in Hallorn?"

"Hiring actors," she replied. *They're trying to get you out of the way*, a treacherous voice said. She ignored it and closed her eyes as the shuttle rumbled into action.

#

Hallorn was a city in the desert country of Holdernay on the planet Alkeemik. Everything was red and dusty and looked a lot like pictures of a place on Earth called "Eejit" that Silver had never wanted to visit, ever. The buildings were hunched shells of metal, erupting from the sand at set intervals, all neat and uniformly boring. Most were shops of some sort and many of the shopkeepers were Alkeemikes – tall, gangly, insect-like beings with eyes on stalks, and facial pincers. Silver had no interest in Alkeemike whores and had no idea why Athanasia thought she would have. She wouldn't even know where to begin... She shook her head at the thought and carried on, looking for likely actors.

Humans walked the dusty streets, as well as other beings. Several languages floated past her ears and she wasn't entirely sure any of it was English. She hurried to keep up with Barkley and the others from the shuttle, not wanting them to leave her behind.

Thoughts of what Justice and Athanasia might be discussing circled her mind and refused to leave her alone, even when she spotted a pretty Jamink girl dressed in silks and entertaining a small crowd. She growled irritably, told herself that it was none of her business – even though it most definitely *was* her business – and caught up to Barkley, grabbing his arm to get his attention.

"Where do I find actors?" she asked.

"You passed them," he said, pointing back at the Jamink girl. "It's all right, you go and talk to them and we'll meet back at the shuttle. You remember the way?"

She did. Vaguely. "I suppose so."

"Good. I'll see you later." He patted her arm and turned away, leaving her to look back at the actors.

She approached the crowd cautiously, slipped in between two Alkeemike women – or what she presumed were Alkeemike women from their complete lack of dangly bits – and watched the Jamink girl dance about on the small stage. Jaminks were humanoid; the only thing that made them appear different were the large, goat-like horns curled against their skulls, and their amber, cat-like eyes. There were more of them behind the stage, working puppets and playing instruments made from animal bones. All of them were female and for a moment, Silver forgot all about Athanasia as she watched, transfixed.

She licked her dry lips and was just about to step around the stage to find someone to talk to, when a hand descended on her shoulder and made her jump. Turning, she came face to face with Captain Justice Jamerson.

"Cap'n! How did you...?"

"I took the second shuttle," Justice said, clasping Silver's hands. "Come with me."

Silver could only do as she was told, as Justice dragged her back through the crowd and quickly behind one of the shops. She was just blinking sand out of her eyes when the captain pushed her back against the metal shell and covered her mouth with her own.

For a moment, Silver kissed her back, her heart thumping. Then, when the captain took Silver's hand and placed it over her breast, she pulled back and looked at her in surprise. "Uh... I don't think we should be doing this." She removed her hand.

"Of course we should, you wanted this," Justice said, grabbing Silver's hand again.

"I used to want this," Silver said, pulling her hand back.

She'd had a terrible crush on the captain back in the day. "But then the whole thing with Athanasia happened... and anyway, you're straight!"

"It's *me*," Justice said, grinning. "Athanasia!"

Silver frowned.

"It's me," Justice said again, lifting a hand to touch Silver's face. "I love you." She kissed her again, but this time Silver pushed her roughly away.

"You've possessed the captain!" she hissed.

"So?"

"So?" Silver repeated. "So? I can't believe you!"

Athanasia stepped closer, her hands hooking around Silver's waist. "I'm just borrowing her body, I'll give it back. Come on, you love this body."

She did love that body. The captain's breasts were so... and her arse was especially... She swallowed. "I can't. It's not right."

"You wanted to touch me, so touch me!"

"Not like this," Silver snapped. "This is... weird. And creepy. This is very creepy."

"I love you, Silver."

"And I love you," she replied, "but I can't do this. I can't. I'm sorry." She gently removed the captain's hands from her waist and stepped away. "Give Justice her body back."

"If you really loved me you wouldn't be able to keep your hands off me," Athanasia said, placing her hands on Justice's hips.

"But that's not *you*," Silver said, exasperated. "Please just go back to the ship, let Justice go and let me get on with hiring these bloody actors."

Athanasia glared at her, lips pursed. The look didn't suit Justice's face, and Silver frowned until Athanasia turned and flounced away. She sighed and walked back to the Jaminks, just wanting everything over and done with.

#

Back on board the ship, Silver presented the acting troupe to the captain – watching Justice's mannerisms closely in case Athanasia still possessed her – and then waited outside the room as the captain had asked. She stared at the grey wall opposite, feeling deflated and tired. Athanasia had vacated Justice's body at least, but what would happen now? Would the sprite take someone else? Or would she let it go?

Silver was just massaging her temples when the door to the captain's room slid open smoothly and the troupe trooped out. She straightened up, smiled when one of the girls looked at her, and then watched as another crewmember led them away down the corridor.

"Silver?"

It was the captain. Silver entered the room and stood before the desk, snapping a salute. "Ma'am."

Justice steepled her fingers in front of her chest. "Good work, Silver. I'm pleased with the actors. They've agreed to perform the play at the price I'm offering and I'll get to see something I've always been curious to see. Thank you."

"You're welcome, Cap'n." She smiled briefly and then moved her gaze to just over Justice's shoulder, her cheeks warming as she remembered the kiss. She waited for dismissal.

"I am aware of what happened on Alkeemik."

Silver glanced at the captain and then away again. She cleared her throat and opened her mouth to speak, but Justice raised a hand.

"Athanasia tricked me and I am very unhappy with her," Justice said. "But, I understand why she did it."

"You do?"

"Absolutely. Can you imagine what it must be like not being able to touch the person you love?"

Silver frowned. "Well, yes—"

Justice waved her into silence. "Go and speak to her at once. Let her know that I've spoken to the tech-techs and they're working on something to enable her to use the hololounge."

"But why would..." She trailed off as the realisation dawned on her. The hololounge was used for recreational activities – snowboarding, horse riding, Quidditch and the like, but some crewmembers used it for less wholesome activities. If Silver used the room and Athanasia was there, then they could... *touch*. She swallowed. "Oh."

"Well? What are you waiting for, girl? Go and speak to her, I have work to get on with."

Silver saluted and darted out the office. She walked back to the engine room, heart pounding all the way; certain people were looking at her and reading her thoughts.

It was cool in the engine room. Quiet but for the whirr of the ancient air con and the hum of the engine. The tube in the centre of the room glowed with a yellow light, and she approached it cautiously, hoping Athanasia wasn't still angry with her.

"Hi," she said, touching the tube. "I have some news."

I heard.

"And?"

I'm pleased.

Silver watched as the light formed into Athanasia's shape, and smiled when the sprite put her hands to Silver's on the other side of the glass. "Won't you be embarrassed?" she asked.

Athanasia laughed. *No.*

"I will be. A bit. I mean, I have to stand there and ask the tender to load the program."

I can load the program.

Silver thought about it and a smile crept over her lips. "I suppose you can," she agreed.

Of course I can.

Silver felt a wave of pleasure flow through the glass into her hands, and she gasped and pulled away, grinning. "What was that for?"

A preview. Come closer.

"Wait." Silver went back to lock the door and then she returned to the tube. She pressed her forehead to the glass and Athanasia did likewise. "I love you," she said. "I can't wait to hold you in my arms." Joy radiated outwards and filled her with warmth. Silver smiled and closed her eyes.

A COLD NIGHT IN H3-II

Juliana Spink Mills

"It's snowing again. Why the *crap* is it snowing again?"

Meryn shook her head mutely in answer to Dav's question. She didn't know why it was snowing again. By their calculations, they should still have the equivalent of a Terran month left of the warmer cycle that passed for summer on H3-II.

Of course, she and Dav didn't call this nasty lump of rock H3-II; they called it something a lot less polite. Almost as bad as the names she called Dav behind his back.

She hadn't been paired with Dav originally. But the colony had dwindled over time until only the two of them were left. Some of the group members had died in a quiet and almost peaceful manner from the Sleep, as they had nicknamed the strange viral disease native to H3-II. Others more horrifically. The mishap at the lava geyser had given her nightmares for weeks.

And now it was snowing again. Not Terran snow, oh no, nothing as soft and fluffy. This was thick, wet, solid stuff that got in their eyes and nose and mouth, and could choke a person to death in a few minutes flat. This stupid, ugly mutt of a moon couldn't even produce proper snow.

Dav came to stand beside her at one of the tiny window slits that provided their only direct glimpse of the outside. He placed a hand on her shoulder. Meryn couldn't be bothered to shrug it off. She sighed, tired of him, tired of it all. She tried to block out his voice, but he droned on and on and on...

"—and the weather cycles are getting steadily worse. Meryn? Are you even listening? Meryn! This is crucial, you know? As soon as we're done fixing the automated feeders in the livestock pen, we have to start work on planning a proper supply tunnel to the dome. If we get cut off we'll die."

I know, you idiot, Meryn thought, but out loud she only said, "I'm going to gear up and feed the animals."

In the airlock, she zippered up her skyshell and let herself out. The storm's muffled howl was a blessed change from Dav's incessant nagging. The path they'd cleared only a day ago was fast filling in, the snow already ankle-deep. Meryn kept one hand on the guide rope, the lights on her helmet picking out the eerie green tint to the heavy, white flakes.

Ahead, the dome was a soft-glowing jewel in the afternoon dark, the farming systems the only splash of warmth in the gloom. She searched the sky, longing for a glimpse of the planet the moon belonged to, or the small, weak star they were trapped in orbit around. But she couldn't even make out the edges of the small valley that housed the colony. Above, there was nothing but a green-grey expanse of cloud cover, and the sheets of wet slush slapping hard against her visor.

Arriving at the dome, Meryn stepped into the airlock. The atmosphere on H3-II was technically breathable for humans, but the colony had learnt the hard way to keep their shells on and their food supply locked up tight. There were too many weird types of airborne bacteria and viruses, like the one that caused the Sleep.

The automatic decontamination sequence kicked in, and she stood under the pressurized airstream until the go-light came on, allowing her to move on. The inner door had a lock code, as did the main building, but they had never bothered to activate it: no point. The multiple scans the colony had carried out since their arrival seventeen months prior had shown no native intelligent life forms.

Inside, the soft hum of the farming systems embraced her, and she relaxed into the scent of damp earth and growing things. She left her helmet on the bench by the door and made her way to the back of the structure, between raised beds of spinach and carrots. Purple garlic flowers nodded beside the exotic beauty of ginger in bloom, and the pygmy orange trees were in blossom. A pollinator drone buzzed by, and if she closed her eyes, she could almost forget about the wintery landscape outside and imagine herself back in the West Virginia of her youth.

She paused to check on the moisture systems, all the lights shining green as they should be. If she turned her head, she could see the dark and empty section they had blocked off when their numbers began to fall drastically and it became no longer necessary or even viable to maintain multiple farm units. It always tugged at her heart to see the bare patches where once life had flourished. She missed the vibrant rows of corn the most.

As she neared the livestock pen, Daisy mooed a greeting. The waiting chickens were fidgeting in the corner, fluffing their feathers. Meryn patted the lone cow first, the sole survivor of the much larger herd they'd arrived with. Like the corn, the cattle had been too big a burden for them once the colonists' death toll rose. She knew they should really think about insemination eventually: calving and milk production, and all of that. But with only the two of them left, it hardly seemed... Well. She cut off that train of thought in a hurry.

She bent down to kiss Daisy's brow and gaze into the large, placid, brown eyes. Sometimes she wished she could swap the cow for Dav. The gentle creature would be far better company. Meryn filled the cow's feed and water dispensers, and collected the day's manure, adding it to the fertilizer processing unit.

She turned to the chickens. The speckled one she'd never liked was acting even weirder than usual, off in the corner staring at Meryn distrustfully. Probably broody. Well, broody was good, right? Meryn stared at the speckled hen, feeling helpless. She knew nothing about livestock. That had been June's job. June who'd been the very first to die of the Sleep, who'd collapsed right here in the middle of the fidgety hens, and who was at present lying out under the snow, in one of a neat stack of metal coffins.

Bloody useless, June had been. Bloody useless, the whole lot of them. And now only she and Dav were left, the most bloody useless of all. The botanist and the communications officer. Oh, Meryn knew all about growing things, and healthy eating, or how to use every last scrap of kale. But all her years of post-graduate study had taught her nothing about moody poultry. Dav was the linguist; maybe she should make him learn Cluck.

She could swear that ruddy bird was staring right at her, its little beady eyes fixed on her own. The hen took a sudden step forward, then another, and Meryn backed up hastily, unnerved.

Chuckling uneasily at her own silliness, she fed and watered the chickens, and locked the livestock pen, setting aside the day's yield of eggs and milk. As she began to do the rounds – trimming and pruning, checking on new seedlings, and collecting ripe and ready produce – she could still feel the hen's eyes on her. *Stupid, stupid woman*, she told herself. *It's just a bird, snap out of it.*

But, as she sealed the milk and vegetables for transit and prepared to exit the dome, she could swear the speckled hen was pressed up against the fencing, still staring at her with its dark, glittering eyes.

#

Morning dawned still and quiet. The mountainous clouds promised more snow, but for now they had a brief respite. After digging out the path to the dome, Dav and Meryn walked the bunker's perimeter, checking for storm and ice damage. The squat, utilitarian building looked nothing like the brave ship it had once been a part of, but it was all they had to call home, sweet home.

The sat dish had been knocked off-kilter, and the wires were a tangled riot. Between them, they managed to take it down and carry it back in. Dav frowned. "Might as well take it apart. There might be something here I can use to fix the animals' feeder system."

He didn't say what she was sure they were both thinking: what was the point of having a sat dish, when there had been no Earth contact at twelve months, or even the emergency-mandated fifteen? They hadn't even managed to get word to Mission Control about the deaths, or the Sleep. By now, it was clear that no new settlers were coming to join them. Considering the dire state of affairs when they'd left, Meryn wasn't even sure there was an Earth left to send anyone into space.

"I don't know—" She bit off the rest of the sentence: *why we even bother*? She and Dav were doing their best to keep things going, to stop the whole failed exploration from falling apart entirely. But some days she seriously considered just going outside into the snow and letting it take her. She gave herself a mental shake. She wasn't ready to prove her family right, not just yet. She didn't really want to die. Besides, Daisy would miss her.

Dav hadn't even heard her aborted comment, or if he had, he ignored her. He spread his tools out on the control room table and settled down to work. Meryn hovered for a while, then left to do some of the other chores. She prepared several days' worth of meals, pleased with the spinach harvest, and ran the pasteurization unit. She patrolled the hallways, checklist in hand, scanning for any technical issues. As she passed through the living quarters, her eyes skipped over the empty rooms, trying not to read the nameplates on the doors. Once this had been a cramped and bustling space; now her footsteps echoed in the quiet.

She went to look in on Dav, who was still hard at work taking the sat dish apart. "I'll do the animals," she said. Dav just nodded in reply.

The wind was picking up again as she arrived at the dome. She peered from the door at the livestock pen, and was relieved to see that the moody speckled hen seemed back to normal. Maybe she'd just imagined the creature's odd behaviour. The forced isolation of colony life with only Dav for company was getting to her.

Meryn walked over to Daisy and reached out as usual to pat her forehead. Daisy was staring at her, big brown eyes locked on her own, eyes alive with a fierce, focussed intelligence. Eyes that were definitely not cow-like in expression.

Meryn snatched her hand back as if burnt and stepped away from the enclosure. Daisy took a step forward, and Meryn could swear the cow *said* something. She slammed the pen shut with trembling fingers, as the cow moved closer, watching her intently.

"Meryn..." the cow hissed.

Meryn turned and fled.

#

"Don't be stupid. Cows don't talk. You're imagining things, as usual."

Dav had his most superior expression on, the one that made Meryn feel five years old. She pulled the blanket tighter, still shivering.

"It was real, I'm telling you. Something's in there, in the dome. First the chicken, now the cow. It's *real*, Dav."

"I can't believe you ran like a little girl..."

I didn't run, Meryn thought. *I applied my intelligence and retreated, like any sane person would.* But out loud she only repeated, "It was real, Dav, I'm telling you."

Dav made a sound of annoyance. "Well, it's too late to go back out there. The temperature is dropping fast and the storm's picked up again. I'll check on the dome tomorrow, and you'll see that you're just being silly."

That night she heard his steps outside her bedroom door, approaching and stopping. She imagined Dav hovering outside, thinking of knocking, and steeled herself to once again say no. But thankfully he walked away, and Meryn dropped into a restless, dream-filled sleep.

#

The storm still churned across the valley the next day. Dav geared up and set off for the dome, forging his way through the fresh snowdrifts. Meryn guiltily watched him go. If she hadn't been so stupid the day before, the animals would have enough feed for Dav to stay inside in this awful weather. Honestly, possessed cows and chickens? How likely was that? Her head was all messed up by this place, that's what it was.

Dav took longer than usual getting back, and she was all twitchy by the time his skyshelled form reappeared in the screen that monitored the bunker's entrance. She refrained from commenting on his delay, though, when he found her in the kitchen. Instead, she handed him the hot milk she'd prepared, cinnamon-spiced and lightly sweetened, just the way Dav liked it. A peace offering of sorts. Dav took a small sip and set it down with a slight grimace.

"Not in the mood today?" Meryn asked, surprised.

He shook his head. "Not really." He looked around, a small crease on his forehead as if he was trying to remember something.

"So?" she prompted. "The cow and the chickens, how were they?"

"Minding their own business. You imagined it, like I said. It happens; I think being out here for so long is starting to get to us both."

Meryn had expected him to be his usual condescending self, but this was surprisingly nice of him. She nodded in agreement. "Yeah, it's been a heck of a year." It came out more subdued than she'd meant, and she waited for Dav's inevitable patronizing response. Instead, he smiled – a bright, cheerful grin. Meryn blinked. She hadn't seen Dav smile in ages. *He should do it more often*, she thought, though there really wasn't much to be happy about on H3-II.

"It really has been a brutal year. Hey, I have an idea." He led the way to the small cosy space they called the media room, Meryn trailing along behind him. "Come on," he said. "We should take a breather. I think we could both use it."

"A breather?" Meryn followed him into the room.

"Yeah, a break. A day off. I could do with just forgetting about things for a while. How about you?"

"That actually sounds pretty good." It had been ages since they'd just chilled out. Since the others had died, things were always so uptight and tense. There were always multiple duties to carry out: housekeeping, repairs, the dome. Checking the experimental stations, though they seemed rather pointless now. "Maybe we could watch something," she added.

Dav flipped through the available titles. "How about this one?"

Meryn burst out laughing. "You hate romcoms!"

He shrugged, looking amused. "Always time for a fresh start." He made himself comfortable on the large, squishy couch and smiled at her. "I think we could do with a lot of fresh starts around here."

His dark eyes glittered as they caught the lamp's glow, and Meryn felt her heart lurch in fright. But then he turned away and it was just Dav, and she knew she was being silly again. She pressed play and sat down beside him.

#

It turned out to be just what Meryn needed. Dav was more relaxed than she'd seen him in a long time and, as the hours passed, she relaxed too. He was actually a pretty nice guy when he wasn't trying so hard to be annoying.

At some point, they got out one of the precious remaining bottles of whiskey and drank to friendship and starting over. They toasted each departed member of the crew, and then they toasted the ship, and Earth, and even H3-II itself.

Eventually Meryn found herself telling stories of her life as a child that she hadn't shared with anyone on the colony ship, not even her intended pair, Omar. About her awful family and why she'd studied so hard to join the one-way mission.

"To get away," she said, hiccupping. "Away from them all, forever, you know? Screw them all."

Dav was a damn fine listener. Meryn squinted at him, bleary-eyed from the whiskey. A damn fine listener indeed. Why had she never noticed that before? And there was that cute little crease on his forehead again: like she was some marvellously puzzling creature he couldn't wait to understand...

Suddenly Dav's face was awfully close and he was watching her intently, and next thing she knew they were kissing. And it wasn't like the last time, all of a fumble and just not very good. It might have been the booze but wow, that man could kiss. Perhaps he'd been practising. Meryn giggled a little and kissed him again.

Dav gathered her close in his arms, and Meryn let herself be drawn into his embrace. He brushed her ear softly with his lips and murmured, "Meryn." For once he actually seemed like some regular guy, nothing like his usual stuffy self. Nothing like it, at all. Warning bells went off in Meryn's head and she pulled back to stare into his eyes. Dav's dark eyes, alive with a fierce, focussed intelligence. Eyes most un-Dav-like in expression.

Meryn sat up, shocked out of her alcoholic haze. "You're not Dav, are you?" She jumped up, stumbling away to the door.

"Wait, Meryn." Dav reached out a hand, but she shut the door in his face and took off, pounding down the hallway, adrenaline kicking in along with the bone-chilling fear. She careened clumsily into the wall as she ran, cursing herself for drinking so much. Behind her she heard the swoosh of the opening door and Dav's voice, no, not Dav, that *creature's* voice calling.

"Wait! I don't want to hurt you. Meryn, come back!"

"Not bloody likely," she muttered, taking a corner at a sprint on sock-clad feet. She slipped and fell, pulling herself up hastily as Dav's footsteps rang out behind her. She dashed into the inner airlock, securing the door behind her, and stuffed herself hurriedly into her skyshell.

The intercom crackled to life. She looked up to find Dav-that-was-not-Dav staring at her through the airlock window.

"We don't want to hurt you, Meryn. We'd like to keep you, to study you. We didn't get to keep any of the others intact. Anyway, where would you go? Come, Meryn, you're being unreasonable."

She didn't answer. Instead, she moved away, eyes steady on the creature, hand fumbling behind her for the controls as she put on her helmet. There was a hiss as the entryway opened, and she stepped through. The airlock shut behind her and she was out in the bitter cold night of H3-II, slogging through the wet sludge towards the only sanctuary she knew. Whatever that *thing* was, she'd be safe in the dome. She could activate the never-before-used locking mechanism and he wouldn't be able to get to her.

The snow-filled walkway seemed longer than usual, her every step a struggle as she battled the waist-high drifts. Any moment, Meryn expected Not-Dav's hand to fall on her shoulder. But she kept forging through, step after heavy step, and finally she made it there to safety in the dome's airlock and collapsed, sobbing. She pulled off her helmet, dangling it from one hand as she ran the other through her tangled, sweaty hair. She flinched as decontamination started automatically.

She forced her shaky legs to stand. She had to get inside. Once she was through the airlock, she could set the door code. She leant on the inner door for support and stiffened, biting off a startled scream. In the dome, staring at her through the window, was a face. Someone long dead. June.

Meryn had shut June's eyes herself, right here in the dome. Once they'd been glassy and empty, but now they were open, lit up with life and intelligence. Other shapes came forward to stand beside Not-June. Mateo, the genius kid from Wisconsin, barely out of his teens. The Australian doctor, Stella. Omar. Cheng. Clarrie. And the others, all of them. They were all there, freed from their metal coffins and their icy preservation, a patient line of waiting creatures, both human and not-human.

Meryn whirled around as the airlock slithered open and Not-Dav walked in. His skin was tinged blue-green from the cold and the snows of H3-II, but he was alive and breathing, even without the protection of a suit and helmet. She could see the plumes of warm breath from his mouth. Was Dav still in there? Trapped somehow in his own body?

"Meryn." He sounded like a disappointed adult chastising an unruly child. "Why are you making this so difficult?"

"You let them out, all of them, that's why you took so long this morning. But how? They were dead?" Her voice was squeaky, small and tight with fear.

"They're not dead, just sleeping," Not-Dav answered.

Meryn glanced behind her at the silent row of colonists,

still inside the dome. Ahead of her, Not-Dav blocked the way out into the night. *Stall him*, she thought. *Keep him talking.* "What do you want from me?"

"We want to study you. I told you so. Your human minds are beautifully complex. So many thoughts and memories, so many *words*." He tapped the side of his head. "Take this one here: visions of a doomed world left behind, of an ex-wife, and a dead son. Hopes for a fresh start and a new life, to be part of something bigger, something important. Fascinating."

"If we're so fascinating, why did you kill the others?"

"We didn't, not really. Their minds are just... at rest. The first ones we took, we pushed too hard and they fell into what you call the Sleep. The animals were easier, no challenge at all. This one, that you call Dav, is a good subject. We took our time preparing and were careful. But you, we would keep as you are. You would be most illuminating. We would take good care of you, protect you, nurture you."

As Not-Dav talked, Meryn forced herself to calm down and think. If Not-Dav and those *things* were here, the only place she could retreat to was the bunker. She could initiate emergency lockdown, buy some time.

"Join us, Meryn." Not-Dav held out a hand once more, but Meryn was ready. She ducked under his arm. Not-Dav grabbed her shoulder, but she slammed a hand over the manual button for the decontamination sequence, and he started as the pressurized airstream blasted him in the head. She twisted frantically and shook off his hand, dropping her helmet in the process. She made a grab for it and missed as it bounced to the ground, but she was out of time. She had to go!

Outside she paused for a split second. Where the heck was the guide rope? Meryn felt around, blind without the glowlights on her helmet. The rope was gone, and the bunker a dim shape in the falling snow.

"Shit!" Meryn's heart hammered in her chest as she floundered in the general direction of the bunker, trying to protect her face from the deadly white stuff. But she must have got turned around, because when the wind dropped for the briefest second she caught a glimpse of the glowing, jewel-like dome away to the right, far, far away, and not behind her as it should have been.

And then she tripped, and suddenly the bastard snow was everywhere: in her eyes, her mouth, her nose. She took one gulping, panicked breath, and choked on it. She couldn't breathe. She clawed at her throat but everything was fading, fading. The night took her hard and swallowed her whole.

#

It was warm in the night – warm and safe in a whispering, gurgling half-dark. Meryn was floating in a pool of water. An odd memory of her mother's voice came to mind, and the whooshing beat of a heart. Was she unborn, then, and in the womb? Or was this death?

Somehow, Meryn didn't think this was death. She reached out in the crimson-black twilight and found... something. Something that was her and yet not her. That something whispered to her tenderly, as a mother to a babe. "Hush, now. Back to sleep. All is well."

Meryn closed her eyes and smiled.

THE COLOUR OF SILENCE

Damaris Browne

Alexi Spencer   Space-dock Alpha   Ten days before launch

Silver and slate-grey; steel and asphalt in the shadows.

The interstellar ship dwarfed the construction dock. From the lower level view-window of the dock's admin HQ, Spencer couldn't even see its bridge far above him. But he could see the tugs slowly manoeuvring Infirmary Unit 3 into position. Workmen surrounded the ship; mechs scurried over its hull. Out there, the relentless bustle of activity. Inside, nothing but silence.

Ten days to wait. Cold strengthened its grip on his heart, his mind, frost encasing him.

The door behind him opened.

"You again?" Batic's coarse voice. "Singh's Earthside with all his cronies, having another meeting with your chief, if you didn't know. So if you want him or his team of ass-lickers, you're outta luck."

Muted sniffing alongside Batic – so Amy Chang was there too, then; PR keeping an eye on the overseer.

Spencer didn't turn from the window. "I don't need to see anyone. It's just a routine check."

"How many times we have to tell you guys? Everything's covered. Jeez. Tightest fraking security I ever set up anywhere, an' I've been doing this since you was in diapers. You wanna knock yourself out, pal, be my guest, but I ain't holding up work so's you an' your gizmos can crawl all over the ship again. Got a deadline here in case you ain't noticed."

Deadline. "I noticed."

"Could understand if you were over at Quayside. Plenty of whackos looking to kill Collinson, and that's where they'll try it. All the media there for the launch, the publicity. Me, I've got a lot less risky ways to kill the prez."

Louder sniffs from Chang. "Security Overseer Batic can get carried away with his rhetoric, Agent Spencer. Needless to say, he has no intention of threatening the President—"

"He knows that," Batic interrupted. "*He* ain't no dick-wit. Anyhow, Spencer, Collinson ain't coming anywhere near the dock nor the ship, so no point your people keep coming here. Unless there's something you ain't telling."

Silence. The man's curiosity burned Spencer's back.

"Went through the lists yesterday," Batic said, voice less abrasive, slyly questioning. "Crew. Medics. Noticed one of the senior medical staff, name of Spencer. Relative of yours?"

"My wife."

"So that's it. Look, she'll be OK. It's a good thing she's doing, going along with the kids, keeping 'em alive till they get to the Kinrintis. A couple of years away ain't nothing. Think of the poor bastards with kids on board, might never see 'em again. Hell, ten days till the last of the IUs are fitted, some of those kids ain't gonna live to *get* on board—"

Chang sniffed her way to a crescendo. "Agent Spencer, I've seen the proposed list for the children for Infirmary Unit 10 which arrived this morning. I know I speak for Security Director Singh and everyone here in expressing our sympathy and good wishes to you and your family."

Another silence, long, awkward: Chang clearly happy to let

Batic sweat.

"I didn't know." Batic's voice came gruff with embarrassment. "Your first?"

For a moment Spencer considered lying: he couldn't bear more pity. But that would be a betrayal. "No," he said. "Our daughter died last year."

Yet more silence.

"No one's gonna try an' sabotage the ship," Batic said at length. "Not even a fraking lunatic would wanna kill all the kids."

"Some fraking lunatic bio-engineered the fraking bacillus which *is* killing them," Spencer returned.

"Agent Spencer." Chang again, trained to avoid and end disputes, emollient, emotionless. "Overseer Batic will, of course, extend his fullest cooperation to you and your fellow agents in your checks. Simply let him know, should you wish to board *The Colour of Silence.*"

Spencer turned away from the shadowed silver; the ice-cold grey stayed with him.

"Crazy name for a ship, anyhow," said Batic, needing the last word. "Silence ain't got no colour."

#

Betinya Collinson   Observation Quay   Launch Day

Grey. Nothing but grey.

She knew her duty as First Lady, so her face was turned to Devon with the requisite look of rapt wifely adoration. Inside she wept tears of ashen silence.

"Ten years I have waited for this day," he said, his voice molasses-thick. His politician's voice. "Ten. Long. Difficult. Years." Deliberate pauses between the words. His politician's pauses. "For all of us." His hands swept round, as if he could gather the crowd into his loving arms. His politician's love.

"Tone it down, Tinya." The press aide's voice slithered through her earpiece. "Devon needs you to look interested and intelligent, not a lobotomised cretin."

She accepted the order, resentment dulled by long custom, and relaxed her expression. Her gaze remained stable, fixed on Devon as he continued speaking, but her hands clenched ever tighter in her lap, her mind frail, buffeted between present and past.

He stepped off the presidential dais, closer to the VIPs and carefully vetted parents who'd been shuttled up to the Quay, closer to the cameras recording for the millions upon millions watching on Earth. The ship with its cargo of hospital pods loomed miles behind them through the Quay's giant windows. A photo opportunity made in Heaven. For him. She was in Hell.

"As my son lay dying, I made a vow." *My* son. Always his, only his. But Sean had been hers. Her joy, her heart, her life. "I vowed I would not rest until all our children were freed from this curse." A silent vow, then, silent as tears. A vow unspoken, unheard, until he first stood for election. "I. Would. Not. Rest." Except to politick. Except to scheme. Except to sleep with the other women.

"And here we are. After ten long years. Ten years of striving. Of success and failure. Effort and heartbreak. Determination and courage. Here we are gathered, to wish a temporary farewell to our children as we send them to our Kinrinti friends far away across the stars. In the hope, in the sure and certain hope, of their survival. Of our survival."

Applause. One of the security team, a tall, lean man, staring at the ship, his face cold, expressionless. Two grieving women being led away by counsellors. Her fingernails biting deep into her flesh.

"When my son lay on his death bed..." Devon's voice cracked, a long-practised trick.

"Sad but brave, Tinya," the voice in the earpiece commanded. "Don't forget, tears in the eyes." In the eyes; in the heart. "Look as if you remember his death." *Remember it?* She lived it. Every moment of every day.

The manipulated cracked voice controlled again: "...my son, my precious son, was full of questions." No. He was full of pain, of screaming agony.

"Questions I couldn't answer." Yes. *Why isn't Daddy here? Where is my Daddy?*

"Among those many, difficult questions was one which held me spellbound: what is the colour of silence?" No. Yes. It was her question. The question she'd demanded while she wept and stormed and raved, her mind shattered, as Sean, her Sean, lay there, silent at last, silent as the grave. Fingernails pierced her skin.

"Friends, this is my answer." He gestured to the ship: his backdrop, his scenery. "This magnificent creation. This new Argo, this new Ark. This vessel of our hopes, our joys, our life. This next stage in the great voyage of humanity. This is *The Colour of Silence.*"

She stood as they all stood. She clapped as they all clapped. She cheered as they all cheered. She wept alone.

She wept in grey silence, red stains on her hands. Colours of despair and blood.

#

**Nirawan Spencer   Aboard *The Colour of Silence*
Eight months later**

Red. Crimson, garnet, burgundy. Dark, dark, red.

The medics were already stripping the cot, the bloodied sheets to be incinerated along with the bloodied body. Another child lost, another family destroyed.

Silence as they worked. Complete silence.

"Doctor. Doctor Spencer."

Nirawan forced herself to turn from the shuttered gurney. "Yes?"

"They need you in IU10, level ten, Doctor."

"I'll be right there."

She walked the long passage between the beds, automatically checking, noting, counting, but once inside the elevator she leaned brokenly against it, trying to hold back the tears, professional detachment exposed for the sham it was.

No longer a doctor, she was a morgue assistant; not a healer, barely a delayer of death.

No.

No, she wouldn't despair. She wouldn't.

She pushed herself up, punched the buttons for 10:10.

Negativity killed. That was the first lesson the Kinrinti had taught them, though one they'd repeatedly forgotten. She'd given up too early, with this poor child, with the others. They all had. They'd stopped trying, submitting to the inevitable. She wouldn't submit, not any more.

They'd learned much in the ten years the bacillus had raged, as they'd watched it change and mutate from child to child, as they'd followed the Kinrinti's advice. Bactericides and tailored antibiotics kept most children stable. A change in oxygen levels had helped, as had the reduced gravity. Children still died, but nothing like the mortality rates back on Earth. They were winning. They would win.

Only ten weeks to planet-fall at the Kinrinti home world and then—

—and then it struck her. IU10, level ten. Euan's ward.

The need to run to him was overwhelming. To run, to hold him to her, as if the love and strength of her grip could destroy the monster ravaging his body.

Akash was waiting, panic overlaid with pity. "Nira, he was doing fine. Then..."

She pushed him aside. Euan's pitifully thin body lay naked on the sheet. The lesions spotting his chest had grown in size, black eschars already forming, but he was breathing. Shallow, weak breaths, but he was alive.

"We've done all we can," Akash continued, guilt, sympathy, justification all jostling for position in his voice and manner.

Nirawan checked the cot readout, saw the cocktail of drugs they'd administered, the prescribed, ineffective cocktail at the fulminant stage. Done all they could? No. She ordered more drugs, changed the mix, increased the dosages, reprogrammed the caterpillar-bots carrying the medicine, ignoring the silent pessimism around her.

More orders. More effort. More love.

She excised the necrotic tissue, the slightest appearance of lesions, destroying the visible face of the monster. Then the final effort.

"Now we put him into the cryochamber," she said.

"But that will…"

Kill him anyway, as it had killed all the children in the early experiments. But the children had been killed slowly.

Ten weeks to planet-fall. Suspended animation would give him ten weeks. It had to.

The medics worked in silence. She watched as the capsule enclosed Euan. Watched as the machine fought the monster for control of his body. Watched as splashes of blue-white appeared, covering the red marks of surgery.

The blue-white spread down his limbs. Colour and hope entwined.

#

Alexi Spencer   Home Apartment   Two days after planet-fall for the ship

White and blue. A band of green at the centre of the planet, some outcrops of brown, with patches of dusty yellow, but mostly white and blue.

No sound, only images. An alien world of ice and sea and silence. A flicker of hope lit in Spencer's breast.

"Wow!" A woman's voice broke in. "Isn't that so wonderful?"

"Yes, Kiku." A picture of the two commentators emerged at the bottom right of the screen alongside the running banner of news announcing what they were seeing. "Wonderful is the word, so, so wonderful. Just to remind our viewers, these are the first pictures of the Kinrinti home-world, being received now, incredibly only days after the transmissions were sent from *The Colour of Silence* as she made her way through the Acesei system, the culmination of ten months of waiting. And the hopes and

95

prayers of the world are with her as we watch the beginning of her descent towards the healing planet, the planet of miracles."

Spencer cut the sound, leaving the newscaster to mouth his platitudes unheard. By infinitesimal degrees the planet grew in size: colour became form, land became contoured. Cities appeared, towers glinting in the sunlight, rivers flashing gold and silver.

The shrill bleep of the com, ignored for as long as he decently could.

"Alexi, are you watching?" His mother was talking before he could speak. "Have you seen? They've arrived. Arrived. He'll be well. Better than well. I know it. Have you heard from Nirawan? When will they get him down to these people? To the healing? Oh, honey. I can't... I'm so..."

"Easy, now," his father's voice cut in. "Let the boy breathe. Alexi, we're with you, son. The worry's ending. Euan will be home before we know it."

But what if he didn't come home?

"We'll have a party." His mother again. "The biggest, most joyful party there's ever been. Honey, come on over, let's celebrate."

"I'm due at work."

"You're working too hard. Double and triple shifts and I don't know what. We never see you. Take a personal day."

"I'm with the First Lady."

"Mrs Collinson doesn't need you, she never goes anywhere, not now she's got so sick, poor woman. They'll understand a personal day. Why, the President himself knows what this means to us. Honey, you heard him. You were there. 'My son, my precious son.' He'll understand."

My son. My precious son.

"I've got to go." He cut the connection.

He ate a perfunctory breakfast, one eye on the viewer, his mind suspended in the ice of clamped-down pain, images on the screen, in his memory, playing out in silence. A red craft approaching the ship; his daughter amid the welter of blood. A pulse of silver as light caught a building; his wife, tears pearled on her cheek. Ink-black shadows passing over the land; his son and the first dark lesion.

His son. What if he could be cured? What if he couldn't?

He dressed with his usual care, drove with his usual calm, worked with his usual efficiency. But nothing was usual. Nothing was the same. They had arrived at the planet.

Snow had fallen in the night; thick drifts covered the gardens. Everywhere seemed renewed, hushed, icy but expectant. Hope was all around.

But hope was the killer. He couldn't allow it in, not again, not to be crushed again by the sorrow.

He patrolled in silence, mind clamping down on his heart's feeble dream of hope. No colour but white in a world of grieving ice.

#

Betinya Collinson   Presidential Palace   The same day

White and orange and yellow. Orange and white of the label on the bottle, yellow of the tablets.

More bright, clear liquid poured into the glass. More burning, cleansing liquid poured down her throat. No tablets, though. They remained in their box, mocking her weakness, as they'd mocked her for weeks now.

Silence, save for an old clock ticking, but then the voice from the corridor seeped from the walls again – from earlier that morning? The day before? The week before? – echoing in her fractured mind. "Already? She can't be. Not at this time of day." *His* voice. Not his politician's voice, not the voice as smooth as the malt whisky she could no longer get, not the *I am your President, I share your pain* voice. That was reserved for people who didn't know him.

I share your pain. The irony made her laugh. Laugh till the tears came.

"Where the hell is she getting the liquor?" the voice demanded... had demanded... would demand. "I want it stopped." *I want. I want.* "Put out the usual statement." *The First Lady*

97

regrets... She did. She regretted everything. "Then get that quack doctor up here to fake another medical to leak to the press."

Another shot of vodka, another attempt to bury the pain. But it wouldn't be buried. It sidled around the drink, its tentacles crushing her broken heart.

But the ship had arrived. Children would be saved. Perhaps she could be saved, too?

She got to her feet, unsteadily, and made her way to the French doors. An agent stood outside. A tall man, lean, with a closed face. He turned as she fumbled at the handle. He didn't speak but opened the door for her.

The air was cold. She stood looking over the gardens, staring without seeing, tasting the chill, the silence.

The agent stepped away, but she knew she'd seen a look of disgust on his face, the look they all gave her. She wanted to shout at him, shriek at him. *Watch your son die. Hear his screams in your mind. Live his last hours over and over and over without end. Then you can look at me like that.*

She moved toward him, mouth already forming the words, but as he turned she saw the pin in his lapel: a miniature ship in silver and grey, its name emblazoned in letters of gold, against his own name, Spencer. Squinting against the light she saw the second pin: smaller, starker, a splash of red and pain. The agent's eyes met hers. Cold eyes. Cold as the frozen air. Cold as the stone that marked Sean's grave. Cold, unforgiving, condemning.

She stumbled back into the room; the door was shut behind her.

The old clock ticked its life away second by second. She counted. Ten seconds and she moved to sit at the dressing table, refusing to look at the ravaged face in the mirror, thinking only of the condemning face outside.

The pills had been hard to get. She'd had to beg for them, one at a time, squirrelling them away until she had enough, keeping them as she wrestled with grief and weakness and hope. She shook them out onto the multi-coloured tray. Yellow against black and red. Sputum and lesions and blood: Sean's final convulsions.

The room was silent now, his voice finally gone, the old clock stilled. She needed silence. She needed to end the screams in her head. The continual screams of a child dying, a mind splintering.

She poured more of the vodka, all of the vodka, then one by one she took up the pills. Tablets of yellow, drink of no colour, shining silver against black. The promise of eternal silence.

#

Nirawan Spencer   Aboard *The Colour of Silence*
Return Day

Black. Black studded with silver.

Nirawan stood at the porthole, staring out into the silence, the cold, black silence of space. They were nearly home, only ten hours away. Ten hours to a hero's welcome, to another ceremony, to more speeches. The President himself would be there to greet them, as he'd been there to see them leave.

He was still in mourning, they said; still scarred by the sudden death of his wife the year before, so there would be sadness amid the celebration. But that was only right. No one could begrudge parents drunk on the joy of their children's return, but they couldn't forget those who weren't returning.

How, no one knew – its microbiome? Its EM radiation? Its minerals? – but the planet had done all the Kinrinti had promised, more than they'd promised. Every child who'd reached the planet had survived. But too many, far too many, had been lost getting there. Images of death weighed on Nirawan, pressing on her shoulders, tearing at her heart.

She thought of all the times she'd stood there, looking out onto the immensity of black silence, seeking answers to the questions which haunted her, seeking a way to live when living seemed beyond her strength.

She turned back to finish tidying her desk. More memories. The guarded, self-censored letters she'd sent to Alexi and their families: messages of love, forced cheerfulness despite the harrowing she daily endured. The unscripted, unrestricted, never-to-be-sent letters where words and tears had spilled from her, cheerfulness left far behind. The reports, the endless unemotional records of statistics and bureaucracy. The terrible official letters to the families of the dead. The wretched private attempts at sympathy which had followed.

Among those who had died were crew and medics. Frailty, loneliness, unbearable sorrow: all had created victims on the ship. Death was the only option, one crewman had written before taking his own life; the only honest option for those who could *feel*. When the blackness had been overwhelming, Nirawan had understood, even once had come close to it herself. But in the end she'd rejected it, as she'd rejected its opposite, the refusal to feel, as she would have to teach Alexi to reject it. Life had to be lived, fully lived, even in the midst of death. Perhaps, at last, he might understand.

A noise made her turn.

Euan stretched and yawned. "Are we there yet?"

"Not yet." She crossed to the bed. "Go back to sleep."

"I'm not tired." He yawned again.

She pulled the sheet over him, covering the scarred chest, the still-thin limbs. "There's hours till we reach home. I'll wake you in time. You won't miss anything."

He grumbled sleepily, but turned, curling himself into a ball, and closed his eyes. She watched as his breathing deepened, as he fidgeted in his sleep, as his eyelids flickered and danced as he dreamed.

The silence stretched, enfolding, embracing, and her heart sang with joy.

The colour of silence? All the bright, brilliant colours of the rainbow.

MY LITTLE MECHA

Shellie Horst

**VOICE RECOGNITION DENIED. MANUAL ENTRY
REQUIRED. YOU WILL BE LOCKED OUT AFTER THREE
FAILED ATTEMPTS.**

"Seriously? I can't fix stuff if you won't let me through." It
didn't make sense. His voice hadn't changed in the last fifteen
minutes. Jared logged the request for reactivation. Thanks to the
archaic systems of Orbital Two, the line of repair mecha was
utterly inaccessible behind a wall of glass. Cool white under-
lighting turned their support frames into a collection of angles and
shadows.

When the panel finally projected the holographic keypad,
he hesitated. What the hell was his passcode? If he'd bothered to
put on his personal environment filter before rushing out of his
quarters this morning, he wouldn't have a problem remembering a
passcode. Stored within it were his personal preferences, so he
didn't have to put up with the station's defaults: his preferred
working music, scenery settings, and yes, a personal log of his
passwords, nestled within the wrist-based system support. "More
haste, less speed," the old saying went; it didn't have to prove itself
true today, though, did it?

"Begins with J, then u?" he muttered, idly trying to invoke muscle memory. "Ah! JsTu5w2R7!" Sure he had it right, he keyed in the familiar code.

DENIED. TWO ATTEMPTS REMAINING. WOULD YOU LIKE A HINT?

"Oh, come on!" Orbital Two's internal system had never responded well to shouting. He sighed and caught sight of his reflection in the glass. He tucked grey highlights behind his still-black hair and smiled into the reflection. Could he bring back that brown-eyed sparkle like the image on his graduation file? He grimaced. No. It just added more wrinkles.

Security hadn't responded. What was wrong now? He pocketed the replacement board and, digit by digit, entered his code. How could he repair the emitter arrays when he was stuck in the corridor?

DENIED. ONE ATTEMPT REMAINING.

It hated him.

"Why? Why? Why?" He banged his head against the cold glass. Beyond the door, rows of mecha and their shelves of modular parts lay dormant.

"How to turn a quick fix into a nightmare." He kicked the panelling, then cautiously tried the code again.

SYSTEM LOCKED. REQUEST RESET?

"Of course I need a bloody reset." He thumped the panel. The decades-old display portal flickered and died. Shit.

Renata would be furious. There were advantages to being married to the station's second-in-command; her discovering he'd smashed the airlock console up wasn't one of them. Nor was getting locked out of the hangar bay. He tapped comms.

"Renata. Need a bit of help. I've a priority repair request—"

"Jared?"

"—but I can't get into Hangar 2."

"Right now?" It was her flat, haven't-got-time-for-your-crap tone.

"All the mecha are inaccessible." He took a breath, then added, "I've requested a biometrics reset, can you speed it along?"

"Biometrics?"

"Didn't recognise me."

"You realise how stupid that sounds, right?" The comm link snapped shut. What was going on? She hadn't heard a word he'd said.

"Where is Commander Başer?" He directed the question at the reluctant system. If she wouldn't talk over comms, then it would have to be face to face.

COMMANDER RENATA BAŞER IS LOCATED IN THE ACADEMY.

Meeting in the Academy? Again? A comfortable lifetime on Earth's Orbital Defence Network, yet she struggled to keep work and personal life separate. He should have expected it. The system projected a route to the Academy level. A green dot represented Renata.

DESTINATION, INNER SECOND FLOOR. ACADEMY LEVEL.

"Get rid of that." He swiped away the route and set off to the residential quarters. As he passed the next panel it beamed an updated projection, his own progress marked with a yellow dash. He sighed. Every comms panel he neared would trigger the same supposedly helpful holographic display.

"Will you stop? I know where the Academy is." He resigned himself to the fact he couldn't get lost on Orbital Two, because a system designed to keep him safe wouldn't allow it.

#

The doors to the education deck hummed open, and Jared again regretted leaving his personal environment filter on the bedside unit. Boisterous tunes and laughter filled the room. Rows of virtual learning bubbles provided a unique sandbox for the student within. To be fair, they offered a better immersive experience than the wrap-around holo-screens he'd been taught on. That didn't mean he had to like them. With so many students at work, it would take an age to find anything. He shaded his eyes against the aggressive neon glow. Without personal environment filters to refine all the personalised learning options, finding

Renata would be hell.

He navigated the sections of educational zones with gritted teeth. If his wife were here, their daughter, Esila, would be in one of the zones. Should he search for Esila, or his wife? A discord of animations and squealing voices screamed for his attention. As he manoeuvred between two of the virtual-education domes, the familiar songs conjured memories of his own school days. The music of learning bombarded his thoughts. Hell, it was vibrant and demanding. He couldn't dial down the assault on his senses. Tunes he'd loved as a child were nothing more than a tailored environment designed to improve his academic scores. All those years he'd thought it was harmless fun. He shrugged away the bitter sense of deceit; it was for the greater good, after all.

Retreating from the noise, Jared looked for a quiet way through. The light around him grew intense. Too late, he realised he'd reversed into one of the virtual environments. The rose-coloured curtain of light around him glitched, then reconstructed its pre-set class.

It took a moment to adjust to the student's augmented reality. He saw what this educational zone defaulted to. Animated butterflies danced across projected cherry blossoms. The sun blazed in a clear sky. Rolling hills of grass rippled in a simulated wind. This cheery female version of Earth was miles from the reality found in the geography files. The intrusion made the student turn.

"Esila!" Of all the environments to interrupt, it had to be his own daughter's classroom. He frowned through the holo-display at the vague outline of adults on the dining platform. Of course Renata would be nearby.

Esila, her hair scooped into an untidy ponytail, blinked at him over her shoulder as he glanced about her virtual classroom. The floor of her learning pod seethed with twitching pony-bots escaping their stables. One ill-thought step and there would be a satisfying crunch of the garish playthings that were connected to her learning program.

Her self-made environment would have been calming if not for the manic music she had chosen to support the game.

Asking her to turn it off would just start an argument. He failed to hold back a sigh. This was karma. He would never leave his environment filter on the bedside again.

"How's today's lesson?" he asked instead.

"Shh..." his daughter hissed. He saw her rows of calculations and shimmering rainbow ponies phase back under her control as she turned full circle in answer. Was he supposed to guess? A silver pony moved to the clop of hooves on nonexistent gravel. The braids in the pony's red mane looked cute. An orange horse followed, its black tail fanned out as it trotted, maintaining a formation she had calculated. The third creature, blue, brought up the rear. There had to be a reason these absurd ponies were being herded around a meadow.

"Algebra?"

She looked at him blankly, then nodded.

"What's that girl there doing?" he asked. Like the robust encoded ponies, the girl was uncannily realistic. She impatiently tapped a foot to the tick of a timer. Dressed in violet, the fake wind tugging at her hair. Esila had captured the flow perfectly. How much time had she spent watching files to re-create that?

"Waiting to ride Nova Tempest," she said.

"Ride what?" He searched her idyllic sky, looking for a nova event. Instead, a green highlight drew his gaze to a purple pony in the stable.

"That's Nova Tempest." The green glow moved to spring up around the unfortunate red-maned beast. "Star Streak and..." With each animatronic's name, stats and calculations overlaid her sky. The highlight moved on to a blue pony as she spoke. "And Luna St—"

She fell silent; she must have spotted the same error he had. He would never know the blue's full name or what she'd named the orange one. He wasn't sure whether to be proud that she'd named all the components of her ED-questria project or be in awe of how eagerly she had thrown herself into the learning platform. What did it matter? She was happy and learning. She glanced to the timer blending into the grasses that masked the taskbar, and her nose scrunched up. When she was three it had been cute. Eight years later, it promised teenage rebellion.

Her soundtrack found an ear-cringing high. Esila didn't flinch; her personal filters were working fine. He couldn't deal with it any more. He reached over her and slid the volume down. Ignoring the frustrated huff, he called up her progress stats.

Green ticks appeared to the left. Swiping through her performance stats, he chuckled to himself.

SUBJECT: HABITAT. CURRENT STANDING: 72%

"Just like Dad." Petals fell into his open palm; her environment specifications informed his senses precisely what she wanted him to feel: delicate velvet.

"Just how I imagined they should be. Yours?"

Her answering nod turned to a shake of her head. "Some."

Jared smiled. "Impressive." Pride glittered in his daughter's eyes before her frown rejected his praise.

"Will you stop?" She wiped the stats into oblivion and reclaimed her world. He'd overstayed his welcome. Messing with her educational environment settings was a no-no. Esila must have sensed his apology, tensing up to reject it. A series of alerts buzzed from the nearby comm panel. Saved by the—

The console lighting tinged her world yellow with warning.

"Need help?" she offered.

"Ignore it."

Her dark eyes called him out on the bad advice. How could a girl still in school help? The Earth Orbital Defence Network didn't trigger alerts for fun, after all. Idiot. No, not an idiot, it wasn't safe. She was still learning how to manipulate toy androids for fun. That's what childhood was all about.

He nudged the blue animatronic pony that lagged behind the others.

"Esila, this pony's too slow." The criticism deflected her attention. "Check your maths. You'll not get them all into the stables in time," he added, assuming it was the aim of this session. It worked; she spun back to her displays muttering something about lunar storms and time. Her focus on the job at hand put him to shame.

Her pinkish world shivered when he left. He missed his

early training in simple, constructed challenges. Nobody actually died there. Responsibility sucked.

"Jared, over here."

Renata waved, all commander and no wife. The education area phased out as he climbed stairs to the brightly coloured dining section of the Academy. Music tinkytonked around them. A different pitch, but it still made him want to stick his fingers in his ears.

"—like Orbital Five, but we'll know for sure in two hours," Renata finished as he approached through the dining benches.

"What'll we know?" He skipped the greetings and perched on the edge of a table. Decades of student names scrawled the surface. His would be here somewhere.

Stood next to Renata, Captain Pete Nonyne frowned. So that's who she was meeting today. Neat Pete, they called him – he looked pristine in the wide-collared grey uniform. Probably because the station-issue garb matched his swept-back hair. That, and his stripes were still brilliant white after all these years. Pete called up the tactical diagram. Though reversed, the projection showed Earth as a small blur behind the dot of the moon. Jared leaned in for a closer inspection. The location of the other orbitals remained in their protective ring around the planet. Three yellow targets didn't belong, and the estimated flight path brought them straight to Orbital Two.

"Those the cause for the yellow alert?"

"Yes."

"An attack? The engine signatures look familiar. It might be the Network's overdue delivery." Jared looked up; she wasn't listening to him. He caught Renata's twitch of a smile, and he followed her gaze. Their daughter fist-pumped the air. Meeting on this level allowed Renata to be a mother while working all hours: multitasking, she called it. There were no rules against it; their parents had done it, and probably theirs before that. She refused to admit she spied on Esila daily. He had to admit the raised dining area was a perfect viewpoint. She would not accept that her priorities, like right now, clashed. Renata wasn't the only parent who did it – he refrained from glancing at Neat Pete – which made arranging meetings a normal, convenient thing to do over coffee.

The captain cleared his throat. Jared really needed to stay focused on the issue at hand, and that wasn't Esila. If the pre-teens on the orbital realised their escape routes were inaccessible with an attack on this scale imminent, there would be a station-wide meltdown. He needed facts.

"How long before they arrive?" Jared prompted Neat Pete to switch the display to a closer visual, showing the increasing proximity of the incoming targets to Orbital Two.

"About two hours. The Network is ready, systems are processing the best reaction." He rubbed his nose and continued to scrutinise the data. "They'll never get through."

"Great." He didn't need to waste any more time worrying about something the Network had been designed to deal with an age ago. "The hangar won't let me in." It was probably best not to mention the broken panel in front of Neat Pete. When they both looked at him, he pulled the board from his pocket. "Renata, I need you to release—"

"Isn't that..."

"Yes, the emitter repair I can't complete."

The captain and the second-in-command shared the same concerned expression. They knew something he didn't.

Neat Pete gestured to the tactical readouts. "We don't know enough. Renata, personally notify the other bases. Nothing gets past this facility."

"Nothing in or out," Renata affirmed with a nod, busy with her own interface.

It was all well and good spouting mission directives instilled in training, but they hadn't heard a word.

"They will without this." Jared held the emitter's replacement board under his nose. "Or you might as well as flag them straight through." It wouldn't be a problem if they'd prioritise the updates his predecessor had outlined.

Renata swiped through screens, not looking up once. "Just replace it." Her fingers flicked through commands. She was already creating a new passcode.

"LM8ebgZm2." The numbers glowed into being as she

spoke. "New code."

"There wasn't anything wrong with the one I used."

She gave him her *I don't believe you* look. "Biometrics are still being processed. God knows how you managed to mess that up."

"I didn't, it—"

Party poppers and applause burst from the education deck. Someone had achieved a self-set goal. Hopefully Esila, but without his personal environment filter engaged, it could have been any of the fifty education domes.

"Did you get that?"

"Yes. LM8ebgZm2," he said, but she repeated them anyhow. Jared pumped the passcode into the notes section of the nearest panel and gave a play salute. "Earth's safe with us."

Her lips twisted in disapproval. "It's what we're paid for," she answered.

True, they'd spent years learning how to deal with incoming threats. Jared had never expected it to become a reality.

Warnings flared up simultaneously from their personal environment filters. The captain glowered.

"This isn't something kids need to be near." Neat Pete made for the steps. "Time to move this to the control room."

Jared watched his wife scan the Academy deck below them.

"Go. She's creating natural habitats, playing with ponies and learning algebra. It's what the kids do these days." He shrugged. Renata still didn't move, though her worried frown faded. "She's safe. Go do what you do."

She regarded him, her lips parting to say something. He shouldn't need to remind her the meeting rooms, security, education offered no protection if the power failed. This was their home; the whole station and the defences it provided could be lost. The idea chilled him. Renata would never let it happen. The summary showed the three incoming targets were advancing rapidly.

"Get that fixed," she instructed, snapping out of whatever held her to the spot. Her expression determined there would be an argument waiting for him after his shift. Fine. This wasn't the place for it.

"Should be all clear in thirty minutes."

Glad to be out of the Academy and its manic environment, he set off at a jog – an almost allowable speed on the busier corridors. Less than two hours before trouble. He could replace the faulty board and be back inside for some family time to celebrate Esila's achievements.

The corridor flickered from soft yellow to a rose hue, the station's polite way of informing everyone to be prepared.

Geez, those ships were moving fast.

#

Locked in the crosshairs, Earth's second orbital station held less menace.

TARGET ENGAGED.

The amber words consumed every pixel – as if she would miss it after all their planning – then faded into the taskbar. The alert initiated the countdown, and with it, the fear everything would go wrong wrapped around her shoulders.

She enlarged the image and reviewed the planned approach on her screens; there was a lot to do between then and now. It was the sight she had wanted to see. They would break through the Earth Orbital Defence Network this time, not just give its systems hiccups.

Raised voices cut into her thoughts. Through her display she watched the captain meet with staff. Time to begin.

"Begin Environmental Audits," she told the system, not taking her eyes from the seniors in the room, "and engage the ED Filters." The last thing they needed right now was interference. If she couldn't focus, her team wouldn't either.

CONFIRMED...OPENING PORTS. LISTENING.

The list of tasks she needed to complete opened to her left. She gathered her dark hair back into a ponytail and analysed the data: minutes until the Network were alerted to her team, distance to target, and fuel were within parameters, but there were still too many red obstacles. Too many distractions around her, not enough hands.

Alerts buzzed in the background; three markers, the red of
S-5, S-4's orange and L-5's blue appeared on the exploded diagram
of the moon's orbit.

"S-5734-RK to N-0VA confirming three on inbound
approach," comms reported, while her Environmental Deflection
continued to process her default settings. The ED revealed S-5's
silver mech: the red shoulder highlights were his trademark. The
burn of S-5's engines muted the stars around him, while similar
feeds from S-4 and L-5 confirmed it: her team had launched.

Breathe in, breathe out. She had this. They *would* complete
the mission.

The deck door hummed open behind her, admitting more
staff. Sliding around her circular dash, she called up her secondary
visual. Stats and video feeds cluttered her vision.

"Keep formation, please, S-5." She dropped the rest of his
call sign. Code names had been her idea at the start of this plan, as
had their vector of approach on the Orbital Network. The best
plans in history changed. She'd take it as a sign.

"Confirmed. N-0—"

The ED alarm found a new level to irritate, and her filter
settings muted S-5's reply before she could interrupt him.

"Hold, S-5," she warned, not letting her focus drift, "don't
want the ED filters to glitch right now." S-5 nodded from the
cockpit of his own repurposed unit. His lips moved soundlessly as
the pixels of her reality glitched and reformed. Someone shouted
her name behind her. She blinked at the supervisor and returned
to her task list. Just what she didn't need.

"Shh…" Her warning faded away; hopefully, S-5 would
understand.

Opening the portal to her N-0 unit, she initiated the power
in the mech.

DENIED ACCESS.

That wasn't supposed to happen. She wrinkled her nose in
thought. If she waited until the supervisor left her team, they
would miss their window. Tweaking the environment settings, she
prayed she hadn't missed anything. She turned full circle to

double-check everything was in order. Satisfied, she inputted the code a second time.

DENIED ACCESS.

The rejection hurt. Why couldn't she connect to the dormant unit? Everything was going wrong. S-5's comm flittered for attention; she ignored it. Their plan seemed all too fragile. The Orbital Network crew must have detected the incoming units by now. She couldn't have them attacking her squad yet.

"Will you stop?" She swiped away S-5's insistent comms request as an overload of stats filled her visuals. Seconds dropped away as the targeting square around the Earth Station turned yellow. The lighting of her console dropped to match. She tried the code again.

DENIED ACCESS.

A cascade of unrequested drop-down prompts cluttered her visuals. Closing them down with a huff of disgust, she glanced across her terminal to where the meeting continued. There was still a chance.

The visual fractalised, shivered, then settled. With it, the ED's proximity alert eased to a less frantic pulse. Alone once more, she allowed herself to breathe. Only that. Lives relied on her to get through the Orbital Defence.

S-5's silent prompt nagged. L-5's comms flickered too. They knew something was wrong.

"N-0, what gives?" S-4 hailed. "I thought we were through?"

"I told you to hold—" she barked at them.

"I'm being hailed by Orbital Five. Should we terminate?" S-5's voice filtered over the soft buzz of his own internal alerts.

"One at a time!" she hissed at them all. The alarm in their voices wasn't helping. How could she concentrate with her team freaking out, their life signs all clearly displaying their growing panic?

"N-0 then, we need an update. What's happening?" L-570-RM persisted.

Nothing. None of her codes would enable the connection to her unit. Not that she could admit that to the team.

"N-0, you said we were clear?" S-4 pressed.

"I'm working on it, S-4."

"Working?" They sounded doubtful. "Are we clear to proceed or not?"

"No. Not yet. The bay is still locked; they still haven't replaced the bricked emitter."

"I thought you said... Oh, God." S-4 was losing it. "If we hit the station and there's no way through, we're all dead."

"*Enough*, S-4." She was in control and S-4 needed to figure that out. "Get a grip." She was barely listening now, tapping in override codes one after another. The airlock hatch wasn't top of her priorities. Perhaps she could work around it? Start at the bottom of her task list?

She switched the display to the hangar. Unlike the three mecha on her visual, the dormant unit's new metallic colour scheme gave it a mischievous appearance. She approved; they were looking for trouble today.

"Sorted it yet?" This from L-5. The blue inbound mech was lagging. A swift analysis of the third mech's systems gave no reason. "Still got alarms triggering all over here."

Distractions were piling up on top of each other; if they'd just shut up long enough, she could scan the audit for another code.

"I'm on it, L-5. Stay in formation."

"They're on to us?"

"Maybe."

"N-0VA, you got this?"

"I do, L-5." What was the point if they couldn't follow their plan, what they'd trained for? "I have a workaround. Give me a minute."

"We've got your back, N-0." They better have: if the attack failed this time, she knew station security would be impossible in future. This was their last chance.

"Be ready, N-0, you need those bay doors open!"

"Will you just stay in formation, stick to the plan, and I'll see this through, L-5."

Terminating the comms felt good. The idiot. Doubt would

be fatal. Follow the plan, or they all died. That's what they had told her, and now it was them dropping the ball. Leaning back into her seat, she admired her own work as the visuals reported back. Everything waited on the final commands. The timer continued its countdown.

AUDIT COMPLETE. NEW PARAMETER FOUND.

The statement came complete with fanfare. She grinned: she'd been right. Everything was in place but her. Completing the connection to the dormant mech would seal her fate and that of the Earth Orbital Defence Network.

"Initiate life support," she said. The processing whirl flickered for an instant before the command was absorbed to power up the fourth machine.

LIFE SUPPORT INITIATED.

Her task list reduced again. Check, and check again, they'd taught her. Would disabling the station be the right thing to do? People lived on it, what if— She shook her head. A bit late for such thoughts now. They had backup power. It didn't hurt to question things, though.

S-4's orange-and-black mech flickered into her lower-right visual, hailing her.

"Your target's locked. Why haven't you commenced phase two?" S-4's fierce face appeared in the lower left. The pilot's hair was colour-coordinated to their machine, brilliant orange with black highlights. She saw their lips twist into a grin.

S-4311's stats were regulation perfect: not even their heart rate showed as elevated. It made her sick that anyone could be so calm. S-4 hadn't got to be squad leader by being green, though.

Of course, they'd lived through it, done this stuff before and helped her through a year of planning. Now it was her turn to ditch the desk and join them.

"Because the supervisor is still chatting to my captain," wasn't the answer S-4 wanted to hear. Her drawn breath didn't soothe her bleeping pulse. In truth, phase two had been triggered by the Environmental Audit. She didn't expect S-4 to understand how Orbital Two worked; it had been her area of study.

"There's a delay."

The feed of the orbital froze. A pixelated image bristled with defences, trained on her three incoming attack-mecha.

"S-4, be aware, the station is on amber alert. The port is still closed," she added, ignoring the alert prompting on her panel.

"We're on final approach, N-0."

And still so much to complete. Target their power systems to create the window needed while the emergency back-ups came online, then deal with the final lock. That's what S-4 wanted to hear.

"They've updated their security," she said instead. "We'll have a shorter window before the emergency protocols come online. Every defence will be targeting you."

"They can see us coming. Don't worry. They won't attack us. They never do."

She didn't share S-4's optimism.

"They chose this, N-0, not you." A reassurance pep-talk from S-4? This was her choice. It wasn't quite too late to turn back.... Some distant report on her life signs must have given away her fear. It wasn't true; the watershed moment had passed. If she aborted now, it would expose everything.

"Copy that, S-4, stay in formation." Everything waited on the final commands. Her timer continued its countdown, but it could be stopped. Once she confirmed, there'd be no turning back.

"Begin the Tempest program." The command triggered more cleared statuses, and her system offered the track for analysis. Sound waves stabbed across her visual. Once she'd silenced the room feedback, the woman's voice was easy to isolate.

Her comm picked the wrong moment to buzz. S-4's display switched to the orbital network warding the planet.

"N-0. Synchronise on my count. 3—"

AUDIO SELECTED. CONTINUE?

The prompt on her control panel glowed.

"2—"

It waited: all she had to do was confirm.

LM8ebgZm2

The system played back the captured code. The personal filter override had succeeded. She met no resistance as she gave her authorisation to initiate the last part.

"1."

ACCESS APPROVED.

Comms with S-4 died. The countdown blurred through numbers.

"It worked." She punched the air as the final red item turned green. The frozen display dissipated, and glaring hazards lit up the workspace.

"Proceed to your dorms. This is not a drill," a female voice repeated. Stunned back to reality, others left their consoles. She fell into the crowd crushing for the corridor. The lights died. Gasps and screams blended into full-blown chaos.

No more waiting to ride. N-0VA was on her own now.

#

Earth's first Orbital Defence Station blotted the moon from sight as it passed on its rotation. Out there somewhere, ships were intent on taking down the station. Jared couldn't see anything, and his mech didn't have long-range scanners to tell him how far off the targets were.

Zoning out the various beeps and the soft whir that kept air flowing through his mech, he nudged the board into place. A moment later the indicator flicked to positive.

"Control: job's done. System test successful." Now Renata could enable whatever she liked. Those attackers had a surprise coming if they thought the Orbital Defence was an easy target.

The repair mech navigated back toward the west hangar on autopilot, freeing his mind to wander through possible treats for Esila. She'd been wanting to control the solar arrays for long enough. Perhaps she'd like that? Nah, she wasn't seven any more.

"Think like a kid, Jared." All he'd wanted was to sit in his compound and chill. Maybe he could arrange something for her.

The orbital's lighting faltered under him, then cut out. Dread pumped through his veins.

INDEPENDENT LIFE SUPPORT INITIATED. THIS IS NOT A DRILL.

Oh, God. All the mech systems were keyed around staying alive; they were the lifeboats, should the Orbital fail. His was the only one emitting a signal.

"Renata?" His voice sounded small. The mech's internal systems unhelpfully tracked his increasing pulse. Time lingered. "Renata?" Her silence was worrying. If he no longer had the might of an Orbital Station to keep him alive...

"Commander?"

His display fritzed, glitched, then cut out. The emergency lighting for the bay crashed out. This wasn't a drill. His systems were down, and it had taken the autopilot offline too. The mech's life support was his last connection to humanity.

Willing himself to breathe, he set off in the general direction of the hatch.

"Jared?"

Renata's panicked voice pierced his comm; his visor readout blurted back into action. Red signals blazed into the blackness. The lighting combination chosen to motivate and warn the other orbitals disorientated him. In the next heartbeat, the station returned to life with full alert lighting.

AUTOPILOT ENGAGED.

That was a start. Though it would be nice if his heart rate calmed too. The floodlit hangar had never looked so welcoming.

"Jared. Our timescale just disappeared."

"Disappeared? How?"

"Don't believe me? Here." His vision filled with trajectory estimations, and the estimated arrival now had fifteen minutes remaining. Renata must have pushed the information across – none of the O.N.D. mecha had the capability.

"Shit." Where had the other hour and a half gone?

"There's more. Esila is missing."

"Missing?" His mech clunked its way through the opening port doors and proceeded toward the hangar.

"Bloody hell, Jared, are you listening?"

It was hardly his fault there had been a complete system failure.

"She's probably with her mates, Renata." If she knew how

able their daughter was, Renata wouldn't be kicking off like this. "Look—"

"Find her before they are in range!" There was genuine panic in her voice. What did she know that he didn't?

The comm clicked silent as the airlock grudgingly dropped into place. She hadn't bothered to ask about him. To be fair, he hadn't checked if she was all right either. She was talking, giving out commands, therefore still alive. No doubt Renata would have come to the same decision. Plus she had access to his life signs. But obviously not their daughter's.

"Locate Esila," he snapped.

PLEASE WAIT.

Jared thumped the mech's panel in frustration. Of course the system would remain isolated until it had completed a full analysis. He couldn't even get out of the cockpit until the all-clear was released.

He drew a breath; venting wouldn't help. How the hell did you lose a kid on a circular facility? Esila had to be on board somewhere. Kids couldn't walk out into space.

He glanced back beyond the airlock door. Had he left the hatch open?

"Come on!" He pulled on the emergency lever, triggering the alarm. Nothing clicked until the systems deemed it safe. His pulse thumped in his ears once more.

The lighting dipped from red to green as the air repressurised. The release snapped open, but the panel was in no rush to lift.

"Done waiting." Using the mech's hydraulic strength, he hauled the security door open. The mechanism screamed.

"Locate Esila."

THERE ARE FOUR ESILAS ON ORBITAL TWO. DID YOU MEAN...

"Esila Başer, *Esila Başer!*"

Processing whirls filled his panel.

UNKNOWN ENTITY.

"What?" The lift down would take an age to reach the dock floor. He jumped clear and rolled, gasping in agony as he landed.

Not as young as he used to be. He used the wall to pull himself upright. "Where's she hiding?"

The machine nerred. He knew the answer: the first place Esila would hide would be the hangar.

He marched-limped down the line of mecha. The last time she'd decided to sulk, she'd hidden in one of the giant machines.

TAKE IMMEDIATE SHELTER.

"Stuff your warnings." The system reprioritised his screen without permission. External statistics replaced the fading search parameters. The attackers were here.

There were no sounds of impacts. Perhaps there was some dialogue happening between sides? Either way, he still had time. Esila would need a mech to get out. That was something. She would need clearance, or the training to use one. No. She hadn't jumped out into space.

Two floodlit bays highlighted empty support frames. One too many.

Beyond the halo of light, a mech stood in the gangway. The whisper of air and the low ohm buzz of power hummed around it.

That thing had moved. It hadn't been there earlier.

"Renata?"

No response. Was the attack underway?

"Commander, someone's initiated the life support on a mech."

"Not now, Jared." The comm terminated from her end. He needed to come at this from a different angle.

"Report unauthorised heat sources."

The system nerred again. He growled. Why couldn't he access any of the basic searches?

"Last update."

NEW PACKET UPLOADED BY NOVA TEMPEST THIRTY-FOUR MINUTES, TEN SECONDS AGO.

Thirty minutes ago? About the time everything started to go wrong. Why did the name ring a bell?

"Who is Nova Temp—?" He groaned. Wasn't that the name of Esila's animatronic horse? The one with a girl waiting to ride?

Bloody hell. She wouldn't dare.

"Esila?" He turned back; the repeating alert gave the mecha an ominous colouring. "I know you're here."

No answer.

If she wouldn't reply, all he could do was lock down the area. "Seal all exits."

ACCESS DENIED.

"What? *No!*"

Bloody biometrics. The countdown to the arrival continued. Each minute would bring a prompt he couldn't mute.

"Authorisation..." Oh, dear God, what was the passcode? "LM8ebgZm2." It took an age to press each figure into the pad.

ACCESS DENIED.

How? Swiping open his notes, Jared stared at the code. LM8ebgZm2. He hadn't got it wrong. "Authorisation LM8ebgZm2," he said, emphasising each number as he typed.

CAUTION.

The word blazed overhead in furious red.

DANGER TO LIFE. EMERGENCY MEASURES INITIATED.

The system was ganging up on him.

AIRLOCK DECOMPRESSION IN 5—

"What? I didn't—" Jared spun. The security partition dropped into place. On the opposite side of the glass panels, the illuminated mech moved toward the airlock.

4—

"Esila?" Pain cramped his chest, but he kept thumping the glass even though he knew... *knew* who it was... *knew* the futility. Knew better. Pressing his nose against it, he couldn't turn away. He had to confirm who was inside the mech. Desperation surged through him. Shoving his screaming fears into a corner, he pressed in the code. His fingers trembled. LM8ebgZm2.

The system nerred at him.

"Esila, what are you doing?" He ripped off the cover of the manual panel. How had she overridden the entire system?

3—

Hell. Esila had been in the room when Renata had given it to him.

"Renata? Commander?"

"What?"

"Seal the port."

"Do it yourself. We have three on attack formation here."

"I'm locked out. She's changed the codes. You've got to stop holding your damn meetings in the Academy." They were about to lose their daughter. He couldn't stop Esila leaving any more than he could speak.

2—

"Now? You want to do this *now*?" Her rage simmered over the comms.

"For the love of— can't you— geez." Panic-induced word vomit stole his reasoning when he most needed coherence. "SEAL IT."

The comms snapped shut. Numbers froze in his mind. The code wouldn't work even if he remembered it. Esila had caused this.

ACCESS DENIED.

Hazard lights emphasised the slashes of violet and purple hues shimmering across the metallic housing. The resemblance to the Nova Tempest doll became more obvious with each strobe. His daughter. Waiting to ride Nova Tempest: the mech, not the pony!

Behind her more lights flickered, the locator signals clear on the three attack mecha in approach formation. One orange, one silver, and one blue.

1.

In the fatal silence, he watched the hangar port fully open.

Why leave now, when they were under attack?

It hit him.

They weren't coming for the station; they were here for Esila. Orange and black, red and silver, blue. The ponies. Gobsmacked by his own stupidity, he pressed his face against the glass, willing it to break. His brain wouldn't shut up with the revelations. She'd relied on their false sense of security, and he hadn't questioned it once.

"Renata." No answer. "Renata, for the love of God! Those engine signatures..." Everything about them screamed O.N.D.

tech. How?

If kids could learn to hack mecha on Orbital Two, what was to stop them doing so on other orbitals?

That fear sparked another. How many other station kids had used generations of parental apathy to jump ship? The incoming formation matched the one he'd seen in her ED-questria. He'd thought she'd been learning. Masked by her environmental filters in the ED-questria platform, he'd watched her plan her escape to Earth.

"Renata." He hated the dread in his voice. He didn't want it to be true. "Did you know?" She still wasn't answering, but it explained her silence. Her constant watching.

The airlock doors yawned into space. He punched at the glass in desperation. The comms clicked in his ear.

"You'll be fine, Dad. Don't be mad." The processors robbed her voice of emotion. "I'm done here. I'm needed down there."

He wanted to argue. To beg. There was no future for her down there. It wasn't safe. The mech's clunking steps were punches to his heart as she ran for the opening.

She leapt, spun and blew him a kiss.

AB INITIO

Susan Boulton

My name is Trent. I don't belong here; I should be back there with them. I did things I can't forget. I had my reasons: Martin said I had no choice, but he is wrong. I did. I got people killed. Silly, really, when you think the Bloat killed 99.5 percent of the world... Or could it have been 100 percent, and we all don't really exist? Just ghosts in our own private hell.

#

Ab Initio. From the beginning. It's Latin. No, I don't know Latin. I have enough trouble with English. Just the phrase jumps out at me these days. Is what I am now doing a beginning, or the ending of something I had begun?

The what-ifs and maybes, beginnings and possible endings are roaming through my head now, keeping my brain from freezing. I wish trying to analyse the impossible would have the same effect on my nose. Damn, it is cold.

The mane of my horse is clogged with ice; each time the creature shakes its head I get peppered with ice barbs. The leather of my saddle is damp with half-melted snow. The rasp of my waterproofs on the thing sets my teeth on edge each time I slip. And I slip each time the beast steps forward. And each time I slip, I worry about the large cylinder strapped to my back. I should have let it be carried with the others. The proof. The salesman's samples that are the fruits of the journey. But I want it close.

Step, slip an inch forward. Step, slip an inch back. The muscles of my thighs are locked solid. I don't think I will be able to stand up for a week after this. As for what lies between the tops of my thighs, well, I would beat a brass monkey, that's for sure. The expression of freezing your balls off has again gained a personal meaning.

Whose crazy idea was it to ride? Mine, of course. Petrol is way too precious. We will need it when we go back for the rest. If we go back. Personally, I don't give a damn. I have what I wanted. Martin, of course, wants it too. He wants to go find the other places as well. Martin is idealistic. He believes in a bright future.

How bloody much farther?

Then I hear it, faintly in the snow-wrapped evening. Ahead of us, we few foolish idiots out for a little winter ride across the Yorkshire Moors. The gentle "hiss-whump, hiss-whump." The wind turbines. In my mind I can see the tall, white towers, the outlines obscured by the falling snow. The blades, turning, hiss, whump. The chill air cut, the power generated, and there the soft glow of home.

Home: a village, a straggling collection of houses that nestle in a valley, where the moor fades out to stone-flanked fields. How long have I called this place home? Not sure; the years move differently now.

"Shit," Eddie swears. His stocky mount loses its footing, as we pick our way through the wind turbines. I glance up, struggling to see these tall sentinels. These symbols of the caring, tree-hugging, early twenty-first–century technology. They were among the first to be up here as a "showcase," to show the power industry was interested in alternatives to oil, coal, gas, and nuclear power. Cursed at the time by many for spoiling the view. Blessed by three generations of villagers since. Things kept the lights on for fifty years when they have gone out for good nearly everywhere else.

"Oh fuck!" I double up, my face nearly in the mane of my horse as it begins the descent to the village. Funny how a single thought can be transmuted to physical pain. Fifty years. I feel like I have been punched in the gut.

"Trent, you ok...?" Sally's knee is knocking mine, her hand is on mine. Leather on leather, the gloves not allowing the warmth of her touch to reach my skin. I straighten up and try to smile at her through the veil of snow.

"Getting too damn old for this, Sal." I cough out the words. Watch my breath form into a small mist and rise towards the wind turbines.

"You're not old, you're barely eighty." Sally tightens her hold on my hands. She, like all her generation, has a different idea of time, life and its possibilities.

"You might not have a problem with that; I do. I need a drink, Sal." I can't quite see her eyes, but know they are narrowed. Sal does not approve of my use of booze to ease the memories. I wonder what she would think if I added I'm dying for a fag.

Our group of intrepid winter-adventuring fools slip and slide down onto the scant remains of the asphalt road. Tarmac, like everything, needs to be cared for. The length leading to the village has had fifty years of not bothering. The drifting snow makes the footing even more hazardous for our mounts, and the string of pack ponies.

I straighten in my saddle and glance back at the bobbing, bouncing mounds on the animals' backs. Thank God for plastic sheeting. Half of what we had found would have been ruined by the weather before we could have reached Harrogate. The last forever nightmare of the eco-warrior is now the protector of the past.

The thought sets me laughing. Sally glares at me through the snow. It is getting heavier. The warm bobs of light that outlined the village are getting blurred. Eddie curses again, and kicks his mount on towards the ditch.

"Ought to fill that in," I say, as I watch the shadowy shape of Eddie swing down from his horse, this side of the ditch. He kneels down, his shape half vanishing in the snow. He opens up a manhole cover, swearing again as the cold metal nearly hits his foot.

"People feel safe with it," Sally says, and signals for the other two with us to dismount and get ready to lead the pack ponies over the drawbridge once it is lowered. She slips from her saddle, and stands watching as Eddie cranks the old field telephone in the hole and swears again, telling the person at the other end to hurry up.

"Didn't your mother teach you any other words, Eddie?" I remark from my position still astride my horse. Be damned if I was getting down. Everyone has to walk in or out of the village. Easier targets, Martin had said. Martin is the founding father of this place. Twice the man I am, a saint, and a bigger fool – sorry, idealist – than any I have ever met, before or after the Bloat. He has embraced the changes in the world, whereas I...

Martin, with four others, had dug out the ditch, some twelve foot wide and fifteen deep. They had used the abandoned JCB digger from the road works in the village, and a couple of farm tractors. Piled the dirt on the inside edge and topped it with a few rows of razor wire. Told me later he had felt like Mad Max that summer, preparing to protect his little bit of surviving civilisation from the hordes of desperate desperados in their homemade tanks.

Thing was, the only folk that appeared from time to time were half-starved individuals that had, like the fifty-odd villagers, survived both stages of the Bloat. In fact, there was enough military hardware lying around to make the ditch and wire useless, if someone had really wanted in.

Forty original survivors in one spot. Hard to believe, isn't it? Genetics? I like to think so. Forty out of a pre-Bloat population of what, a couple of thousand? Not that that percentage survived in any of the big cities, I swear it, or if they did, they did not last long in the horror years. I would guess that the present population of the UK is roughly 975,000 or maybe a million, and there is what, over three hundred here in one spot, pretty impressive. And every one of them bright-eyed by the future in front of them. The rumble of the drawbridge cuts through my thoughts, and I kick my mount on. The beast, sensing its stable, snorts and breaks into a stumbling trot.

I leave my horse in front of the stables, the converted row of garages behind the old council houses on Briar Way. Let the others deal with it. Age does have a few perks. I stumble my way towards my quarters, cursing the fact that they would be cold. Power was for lighting, and other necessary items, but not for heating houses, least not those on the outskirts of the village.

Perverse? Well, I like living alone. Don't like to see myself reflected in the eyes of the "younger generations." I could have a room in any of the houses. Martin is always nagging me to move in closer. I think he is afraid I will be found choked to death on my own vomit, or hanging from a beam in my cottage.

You see, he worries. Good reason, too. I, more than any other of the survivors here, find it hard to come to terms with what the Bloat took away and gave. Maybe because of what I did in the name of preserving the past.

For Sally's generation it is "normal," this strange blend of bits and pieces of technology, this existence in the shadow of the Bloat, and the prospect that they will live, how long? That's the rub, isn't it? No one knows yet. But they see it as a wonder unfolding before them. So much to see, so much to do, and plenty of time to do both in.

I stamp my feet on my doorstep, trying to regain some circulation. Push the door open and... there is a glow of a newly lit fire in the hearth of my living room. Was a figure sitting in one of the winged chairs?

"Welcome home, Trent."

"Bugger off, Martin." I slam the door.

He chuckles, and switches on the small lamp on the table by the arm of the chair. I ignore him and pull out the plastic-wrapped tube I have carried on my back since York, and place it carefully against the wall. I strip off my waterproofs and boots, leaving them in a wet puddle, as I go upstairs to find some dry socks. I sit on the top step, pushing my cold feet into a mismatched pair of woollen ones. Martin stands at the bottom, a glass of something in his hand. He swirls the liquid and takes a sip.

"Hell, is that my single malt?"

"Not bad," Martin replies, as his smile widens.

"You are a sod." I stand and come down to him. We are of a height, both of us an inch short of six foot. Martin was forty-five when the Bloat began in 2020, nearly fifty when the full effects of it began to dawn on the remains of humanity. He is what, a hundred? And looks not a day older than he did when he came to after the Recurrence, as it was – and still is – called. The second bout of Bloat, or rather the second stage of the illness that took the one thing that had driven humanity to create much of what we have brought home with us.

Me, I am nearly eighty, going on thirty.

"Sal give you a hard time?" Martin asks, as he moves back into my living room.

"Pain in the arse," I mumble, and make for the bottle of Glenmorangie. The pale golden liquid shimmers, as I pour it into a glass. The liquid had been fifteen years old when they put it in this bottle. Another fifty hadn't harmed it. I take a sip. I want to guzzle it. Martin knew it. That is why he had pulled the Glenmorangie out of my store; he knew I wouldn't waste it to get drunk.

"That's my granddaughter." Martin chuckles, and sits again by the spitting fire.

"That's the problem. She is your granddaughter."

Martin leans forward and swirls the liquid in the glass. "Age doesn't mean the same thing now."

"It does to me," I snap, and against my better judgment and regret, empty the glass in one gulp.

My hand shakes as I pour another drink. The final part of the ride over the moors has exhausted me. No, the memories have.

I had promised Martin I would take a party there one day. A day when we had a place suitable for storage. He felt it was important to preserve the past. The whole community did: it was part of their plans for the future.

We have the perfect place now.

So no more excuses, I had to go.

"You have some explaining to do," Sally says sharply as she

comes into the room.

I lift my glass full of golden liquid and look at the young woman through the soft swirls. She is just over five feet, curved in all the right places, strong of limb. No one here has any excess fat: the hard work of surviving takes care of that. As for her face, she is nothing special. If I were cruel – no, scrap that, I am cruel. Sally saw part of that cruelty in York.

Where was I... yes, Sally. God, take her piece by piece, it is hard to find anything attractive. Yet put them all together, with that mind of hers shining in her grey eyes, hell, easy to love, too easy. Oh, don't get the impression I am being noble or anything, I would have no objection if it was just, well, just. But not with Sally; I had watched her grow up, felt her become part of my life. I couldn't. I fell back on the "age" thing. I cannot bear the fact that if I allowed her in, became the husband, father of her children, everything she has set her course to do with me, I would destroy her.

My past will destroy her. It's out there, still alive, still hunting me. My years here have been a respite, nothing more. I am still bound by the one thing humanity had lost. I tear my mind from the past and say jokingly, "Sorry, next time I will unsaddle my horse."

"That's not what I meant." She begins to strip off her own waterproofs. A small lump of snow falls on her left cheek and melts, running like silver tears. I lower my glass, and look back Martin.

"I know, it's what we found at York, but it is not important."

"Not important! You must know what happened there? The first doors were locked, barred, then the airtight doors, but between them, the passage, you must have known what was waiting for us."

"Pray do tell," Martin says, softly.

I put my glass to my lips and drink, spilling the single malt down my chin as I gulp it.

Sally glares at me and goes over to her grandfather. She goes down on her knees and takes his right hand in hers. "It was..."

She looks once more at me, then sighs. The sound shakes her body, and she begins to speak – flatly, no emotion, but the lack of it, the forcing her voice to be toneless, makes my stomach roll.

"Trent had said York was bad. I didn't think it would be worse than Harrogate or Skipton, but it was. A maze of half burned buildings, roads so clogged that... At one point I didn't think we would get to the Minster. But Trent knew a way, didn't you?" She looks round at me. I don't answer, just refill my glass and move to the other chair by the fire. I slump down in it, my legs out, head back, and my mind fifty years in the past.

The Bloat: where did it start? I don't know. I don't think anyone knew. Hell, those of us that survived have talked the subject to death for fifty years. It was a virus; well, they thought it was. The authorities never really let on. Some said that was because they had created it. Personally I believe they didn't really know. Look at AIDS – how long did it take for that to become known. CJD. Ditto. And all the hue and cry over both, and the Bloat was waiting in the wings.

Do you know what your lymph system does? It is the filter system for your body, a big part of your immune system. It is made up of vessels and nodes which, with the aid of your muscles, pump the lymph round. It clears out your system and fights disease. A healthy lymph system means you are healthy, you don't get sick very often, and you can spend your life making a prat of yourself.

A damaged lymph system, one that is not pumping right, means that the lymph is squeezed into the surrounding tissue, and with it, all the crap that it is supposed to remove. So your leg or arm or body swells. The limb becomes heavy, painful, red, swollen. Then it's feeding time for any other virus. You are one big lunch box for septicaemia, gangrene, and all their other little friends.

So imagine one day your lymph system saying, "Bugger this." And just stops working. Now with a damaged lymph system it takes a while for your limbs to swell. With the Bloat it was twelve hours, and you were like the Michelin man. The virus had shut things down for its own purpose. Within the next twenty-four hours you were either dead, or slowly, weakly, realising you were still alive, and your lymph system had, for the same unknown reason, started again.

Now it took two years for the Bloat to munch its way round the world, and it left half of the world's population dead. That's worse than the Black Death in the thirteenth century: Europe lost a third of its population then, but it survived. So did we, we thought. Things were a mess, but you still had power, TV, and the internet, so all was well with the world.

The crunch came about three years after the outbreak. Seems it took three years for the virus to finish its work. Nice little job it did, rebuilding your lymph system, rebuilding you. Steve Austin the bionic man had nothing on us. You see, the lymph aids the body to repair itself, and fights infection. So what if a little bug decided to redesign the cell structure, and then the cell structure slowly redesigns the host.

Why? Well, my guess is the virus wants to live, needs to, like the rest of us: maybe it is a symbiotic virus; it needs a living host to live happily in for ever and ever.

One chap I came across had this theory of spontaneous evolution. That a mutation can occur suddenly, and change a species overnight. He was convinced that was what had happened. We were the next phase in human evolution and it had been adapt or die. The old survival of the fittest. Well when you look at it, it holds as much water as the grey aliens doing it by putting genes into us that didn't belong, the X-Files conspiracy, and what was that, oh yes, government created little tiny bits of nanotechnology that had gotten loose. Nah... too much Michael Crichton and whisky.

What was it; oh yes... the Recurrence. The Bloat virus, or little bit of micro mechanics, the alien gene whatever, had spent a couple of years reprogramming you. So what else, like any other computer, even one of flesh, you had to be shut down, and rebooted. Big problem: most didn't restart.

Re-start.

Re-boot.

The hitch in the breath.

The pounding of the heart.

The screaming of the mind.

"You knew!" Sally's accusation cuts through my brittle memories. I bring my head up and look at the young woman on her knees before her grandfather. Her face makes my heart ache. Damn her. I don't want to explain. Tell what I had done.

Martin is sitting there, one eyebrow raised, a small smile on his face as he speaks. "What did you find?"

Sally looks at me, capturing my eyes with hers. "Bodies."

"It was the middle of York, Sal. Folk just dropped down and never got up again; bound to be bones lying around," I mumble.

"These were nailed to the wall in the passage: three of them, what remained of them. Others, God knows how many, piled against the door of the safe room like a barrier."

"Ouch, you mean nailed as in hammered? Hard work, that," Martin says.

"Actually I used a nail gun," I say.

"They were dead from the second stage, right? You did it as a warning, mimicked the gangs that roamed the cities in the horror days?" Martin says through Sal's gasp. "Make it look as if it was a no-go area?"

"Partly; they were dead, the ones piled against the door right enough, but the ones on the wall, *nailed*, well, they were alive, or at least not quite dead, when I did it."

"You killed them?" The horror in Sally's voice tears into me.

"I had no choice, the bastards would have done me in the moment I opened that place up, that last time."

"Why?"

"Why, Sal? You saw what was in there."

"Art, pictures, sculptures, computer discs, jewellery, everything we need to preserve from before the Bloat."

"Exactly: a fortune, neatly labelled and stored away in a sealed vault."

Martin shakes his head. "What did they think they could do with it? Set themselves up as kings?"

"Oh, Conner, that was his name, had a bright idea, convinced others of it too. He believed the Bloat was limited to the

UK."

Sally shifts closer to me, her hand reaching out and touching my knee. *Don't, Sal, please...* my mind whispers. "He had contacts, he said, in the US; they wanted the contents of the vault. You know it took me and..." I let the words fall away, and I think on the rolled-up picture in its container in the hall of my home, here.

I can remember it so clearly the first time I saw it as I prepared to pack it away for preservation. It was the early summer after the Recurrence began in earnest. Hell was open and we, the world, had been tipped in. Martin was thinking about digging his trench, and I was trying to save the beauty that had been put on canvas. It was my calling. Well, actually, it was a last-ditch attempt by the ragtag that was the government to save something for the future. I was one of a motley group of thieves going from art gallery to stately home, loading up items and taking them to "safe places."

Back to the picture. I stood in the Fitzwilliam Museum in Cambridge, fifty years ago, looking at it, and I began to laugh. The whole cosmic joke of the Bloat dawned on me, as I helped lift Salvator Rosa's *Human Frailty* from the wall. Art historians waxed lyrical about the seventeenth-century symbolism with regards to birth, death and everything in between contained in the picture, but for me it was, and still is, the hand on the child's arm. Death in winged skeletal form, taking possession. Not removing the child from its mother's lap, no, just the lightest of touch is enough.

I still am laughing inside.

The picture is us. The past us. The part that the Bloat has taken from us. Something those born after it will never know. Illness no longer exists. Oh, you get a mild case of the Bloat when you hit puberty, and that is it. Barring accidents or, in the case of those I pinned to the wall in York, murder. Humanity has lost the very thing that drove it to produce the artefacts Martin wanted to save. Humanity is no longer frail. It no longer fears the very thing the artist strove to show in his painting. The very thing that drives me to drink. The loss of what has made us so human, our frailty.

I look at Martin, then at Sally. Her expression has softened. Have I been granted absolution? Has she seen my frailty? She reaches up and gently touches my face, and yes, maybe she has. And maybe she understands.

THE SHADOWS ARE US AND THEY ARE THE SHADOWS

Jo Zebedee

It's the last of days. We've screwed Earth so badly that we have to go. No matter that we have no habitation set up on New Earth. No matter that successive governments failed to deliver on their promises. They didn't save Earth, and they didn't provide us with an alternative we can live on. All we have are the ARK ships, ten of them, distributed across the world. We're told they're reliable, that they'll carry us to New Earth. We're told the supplies are there for us to thrive, but we don't know. Not for sure. Because politicians lie all the damn time, and this time they might lie more than ever, now that there is nothing at stake but their own pride and legacy. The lies we tell ourselves are sometimes the strongest.

I load supplies into the galley, my allotted job. The air tears at my lungs and I should be used to it, but I have to stop to draw breath, wheezing it in, eyes streaming as I cough. With one ear I listen to the crackling radio, broadcasting over old frequencies now that everything that was SMART is offline. Humanity stretches over the Earth, but we are barely connected anymore. I like it, in its own way. It gives me time to think.

The second ARK ship is ready for launch. The first left yesterday, from the Siberian plains, the Russians winning the ultimate space race. It went up, as planned, giving us hope. Some humans are already in the skies and free from the planet.

The countdown begins, the dead tones of its mechanical voice cut by static. What will it be like, to be inside a ship when this happens? Will I be stoic and brave? Or will I shit myself and have done with it? Christ, I hope I don't. Tenza Newman's last gift to Earth: a stench and a fart. It would be my luck.

The countdown hits three. I find my lips moving, a prayer to those on board. Selected, so few of us, the future of Earth. I feel as close to them as any Web-link could have made me. I feel they are my brothers; my sisters.

The engines' noise, carried all the way from Australia, fills the air. Everyone around me is still now. None of us dares to speak. Magson, my pair-bonded, stands, his hands clenched. I like him well enough, his pugnacious manner, how he fights and doesn't give up. Don't fancy his looks much, but I doubt I'm a picture. Not on this barren Earth, with a body that's parched from years of thirst, of scorched air; that has dirt engrained in every line; that stinks of sweat.

"They're up," says Jammer, beside me, and they are. I imagine the rocket arcing over the land, over the sea, reaching for the stars. Imagine the thrusters breaking off, the engines taking over. Imagine the people on board beginning to relax, even as the gs press them to their seats. Magson's fists uncurl. I reach for the next box to set it into place.

A brief snatch of sound, a dented explosion, stops me. The cries on the radio, the keening, the broadcaster's crinkled voice trying for calm, but the message is clear. ARK-II has failed. There will be no Australians on New Earth.

"Well, shit," says Jammer, and he has it nailed.

I load my boxes and try not to think that in five hours, that could be me. We are ARK-X: we will be the last to leave this planet. And we may not make it through the atmosphere.

#

During the day, we dig. Underfoot, rocks shift, loose in the barren ground. Nothing grows here. There's no water, so far from the plains. Only we grow in this barrenness. We do not need water to work. We do not need plants to eat. We can survive in this red land, in the dusty air that hazes our eyes.

Sometimes it's easy to tell what items we have found. A receptacle for holding things; a blade that's sharper than any we make. Others get passed from one of us to the next, and we try to guess their purpose. A tube of thin, clear plastic, light in our hands. Did it hold a blade? Or did it have a purpose we cannot even guess? It's a game – of sorts – but more than that. It connects us to the past.

Sometimes, we find an object that is *more* than the others, and we tell tales about it. Some are true, passed from the Founders, but some are created in our imagination cells. It's the not knowing which is which that keeps us real. Storytellers are real. Uploaded minds are not.

A large section of metal, splashed with colour, is one piece we argue over. Our Mother-tell tells us it was part of an iron bird, the type which the Shadows left Earth on. I touch the metal and don't see how it could be. Birds had feathers. There are pictures of them. But Mother-tell is sure, and it's hard for me to understand the truth.

That's all for later. For now, under the sun, I turn over the next bit of ground, and the next, until something new appears. Glass and metal are best. We can do something with those. The bits of plastic, colours bleached and sick, are useless. They can't be reshaped. Often, they'll be partially broken down so the plastic is brittle and no use for anything but to be discarded, again, where it will leach into the soil further.

Today, though, is better than glass-metal. Better than a flying Shadow-bird. Today, I strike gold in a white glint of bone. It's old, but the half-ruined fabric that falls away tells me it was human.

I shout out. The team join me: we dig and shift, dig and shift, quickly but with care. At last, the whole body is revealed, and it's intact. A miracle in the making.

We make a shroud and carry the body between us, taking care not to rattle, or damage, or disturb. As we walk, we sing of the Shadows, a low song of fear, and hope, and blinding pain. The red dust is all around as we walk, and we have a body, and so I believe the day is good.

#

Of the ten rockets, three have failed, six have left the atmosphere, and one remains. Ours. ARK-X. The first built, here on Project New Earth's base, and the last to leave.

Of those that left, we have heard nothing, and will not. I will never know how many of Earth's people we saved with these botched-together rockets. I will never know if those we save carry a next generation forwards. I will never know if New Earth could have sustained us.

On balance, I prefer it that way. It lets me focus on the moment, on what I need to do. I cross to the Genesis-Room, leaving the rocket behind me.

Inside, five of us meet, each with a key in hand. We are those who devised this plan. We are those who will enact it. In front of us, the AIs wait, idle, needing their programming. They will continue our work. They will cleanse the Earth we have ruined.

Jeff built the interface between the AI and the robot-body. He focuses on function and assimilation. Diane is about hardware, ensuring that each AI's metal body can endure the wasteland Earth we leave behind. That they are tough enough to survive attacks from those people left behind, who will surely madden as they sicken and die.

Margaret watches the screen, checking the diagnostics of the life-systems that will sustain this small army. She's our details go-to, the overseer of all. And Duv; well, Duv owns nothing but the idea. The crazy idea to leave the Earth, let it die and be cleaned and renewed by these AIs so that our children's children, their children's children, however many generations it takes, may return.

But he does not own the coding. That is my domain, and I struggle daily with what I ask of these AIs, who are the children I will never carry. Do we have the right to demand they carry out our will? Or should there be more that we leave behind, a last legacy of our thinking race, held in the tech pods? Perhaps, if given the chance, they will be better than us. They could hardly be worse.

"I have some final checks," I say, and sit in the seat before my terminal. Can I do this? It will be monstrous. And yet my fingers dance and I input my hidden command, strike its title onto the screen: LIFE.

I step back. Lift my key. "Ready."

We each assert our readiness. We turn our keys. The AI lifts its head, looks at us, and we flee. I can't tell if I'm running from its judgement or the dead Earth itself. We flee onto the ship, strap in, look ahead and not back. The countdown is louder in the rocket than it ever was on the radio. Magson stands opposite, and he's grinning, the crazy man. I like that he's mine, that he has braved life. I like that he's not scared.

The rockets bloom. The ship rises and I know this is never going to work, that the ships will never survive two generations in space, even if they have got through the atmosphere and into space. We will never carry enough children for us and even if we do, what of them? They won't be Earth children, but something else. They may never be able to return; they may never want to. And yet I hope, because a lifeless Earth is no Earth at all.

I'm still thinking about it when the first alarm sounds, when the dull explosion buffets the ship. I grin as blackness takes me, high over the sky, where the ship will be scattered and strewn on Earth, where it will hit with such force it will be buried and lost for years. Decades, perhaps. Aeons, I hope.

#

The cry goes up as the watchers see the shroud. *A body! A body.* The calls rise into the air, becoming louder and louder. We wait, letting the crowd grow, until the moon comes up. It's a broken one, shrouded by the ash that litters the atmosphere, but we gather together what we must, and it ends up mostly intact, with only a few, non-essential, bones missing.

Tonight I am the central skim, the one that matters. I found a body, left from a metal bird. I give us hope. My arms reach for the moon, grinding metal on bones, my shirt flapping, and I rejoice.

We unearth our cache of metal. A panel, paint peeling. It's so big that it must be more of the metal bird. I wonder if they ever sang further than this planet, and if the Shadows watch for us. This is not a good thing to think about. It makes me shiver, makes my skim feel thin as if the cold could get into my bones, but still it's there, the fear: what happens if the Shadows do not watch?

A new shout goes up. We have enough metal. We will make heat from the mother-source as the sun rises slowly. That's its way. To fall quickly and rise slowly, through smog-filled skies, to illuminate a world that's barren. Perhaps it is ashamed of its child. We match its rise with our chants and dream that one day it will love us. See what we are doing, how we are fixing things, we plead.

A clattering noise announces the arrival of the panels, drawn across the land during the night before, shared between emplacements. The cart makes its way slowly, hands on each side to steady its treasure, more hands on the panels themselves. When it stops, I go forward and I stroke the panels and marvel at them. I've never been allowed close before.

The solar panels are set in place and turned to the sun. The emplacement that last held them will have done this every day, maintaining the charge. A heartbeat's breath is held in me, and then the hum of life comes. Soon, a great searing heat, so that I step back to save my skim. More of the sun has been revealed over the years, the ash-cloud stripped back as we have mended and fixed and worked.

With a low song, a prayer for the dead, we load up the metal pieces, into the channels heated by the panels. It twists and turns, its shape blunting as it melts. The metal forms runnels, following pre-laid tracks into the trough awaiting it.

At last, there is enough. We place the body, allowing the shroud to sink into the metal. It flares, a brief flurry of light, and then the metal welcomes the body, embracing it, consuming it. All around songs rise, words vibrant, and I am the one who stands closest, who watches the last bone vanishing.

At last it is done, and the stolen body lies still. But there is no life. We keen and call, until Father-life makes his way through our masses. To some, he says a word. Others, he touches a limb. Some he moves past, giving no comfort for none is needed, until he reaches the coffin. He moves me to the side, but I still stay at the head of the crowd.

Father-life bows his head. He touches the trough and, although his skim must burn, he doesn't flinch.

"Unknown," he says, and he caresses the name and it doesn't matter that this person is not known, for with us they will be. "We thank you for your sacrifice."

A murmur runs through us all.

"We thank you for your gift, for emerging to the light." No mention of the digging that brought the body to us; to dig is to find, to find is the gift.

"We give thanks that you are complete."

We give great thanks for that. One cannot become two; two cannot be made from one. We maintain, not expand.

"We welcome you to our midst." He presses his fingers against the metal, and puts his head back, eyes closed, lips drawn back, and holds himself thus. Long moments of hope pass, but I am fearful. What if I did not bring life, but something useless? Old bones that will not take? It happens more and more these days, as the bones crumble in the dry ground.

A stirring within the metal makes my skim tighten and ripple. The murmur of the crowd. In the redness, silvered eyes open. Our new body takes the life I have brought it to.

"Now you are as a Shadow," declares Father-life. Mother-tell joins him and they bring the new person forward, bones melded, metal skim encasing it. She will take this story of a new Shadow to emplacement after emplacement, bringing it to the Oldest Land, where Grandfather-call waits. His beacon stays silent, none of the light that has been promised. The Earth is not yet healed; we have not yet done enough.

"The People have left us," says Mother-tell. We crowd forwards. We know the story, but still we listen. She touches her own head, and we do ours. In there, the chip that allows us to be. "They left us to maintain their Earth, to hold it in trust. We were the People's children."

Her voice lowers, becoming a caress. "We were their Shadows." She touches her body, and I touch mine. Inside, we are bone, once alive, not dead metal. "This is the Earth's gift to us! Humans weren't made so because of their body. Why, the animals and the fish had bodies, too. Don't we dig up their bones?"

We shout, "Aii!" We do, often, bones in the sand, bones in the rock, etched pictures of fish made by their bones, small fragments of delicate bird.

"Beetles and insects that lived on this planet had bodies! But they did not have thought. They did not have synapse."

Our new-born is helped to stand by me. Already its synapses will be flaring, already their programmed chip will be responding to what it is seeing. It will be taking the knowledge held in the bones and merging them. A new person will be born, not a computerised chip that only thinks one way.

"To think is to be human!"

We inherited the People's thoughts, stored on the chips in their tech-pods.

"To be independent is to think!"

And we are independent. This emplacement came together; others have their Mother-life, and Sister-light. We are who we choose to be, just as I chose to dig, to have hope to bring this life. My eyes grow hot. Had I water, I might have cried. Had I food, I might have retched.

"We are intact, in body and thought!"

Father-life has drawn the newcomer forward. A female, by their look and size, but who could know for sure. Father grasps his hand to her hand, welcoming our newcomer to the emplacement. I remember that moment in my own creation. The shock. The bio-memory of my bones and then the sparking knowledge of the implant. I understood the past and the future, what was demanded of us. I remember my first thoughts, how I rocked with what was demanded of us.

"We are not the Shadows of the People," cries Mother-tell, close to the ecstasy of the moment. "They are our Shadows, for they do not live!"

The New beside me coughs. She clears her throat. Her first words will emerge, the proof of the miracle.

"I am Tenza Newman," she says. "I am the architect of thought." Her eyes flash. I back away. As one, we fall to our knees. Tenza, whom we have sought through all our generations, who will ask our decision on the Shadows, and follow our will.

Tenza, our creator.

"What will your wish be?"

Mother-tell and Father-life stand before the creator. My, how straight they stand. How brave they are.

That this should be our colony's decision. I could never have imagined so. And yet, the decision is all the AIs, discussed and agreed. The sunlight falls around us, cold and white and hard but still warming the exposed Earth, bringing life back inch by inch, plain by plain, mountain by mountain. This is our job, and it is a good one; well done and worked, and we are proud, Shadow-Babies that we are.

We begin to sing, the words we have practised since rebirth. We sing it for Tenza, our creator, who gave us choice and freewill.

Our song reaches its crescendo. In the centre of our world, Grandfather-time will come to life, the guardian of the communications to the stars. He will reach for the communications command, and he will send the word across the stars that will bring Earth's people back.

I sing. We have chosen right. We have performed our task to perfection. Now we must complete it, and give Earth back its life.

The Shadows are us and we are the Shadows.

ABOUT THE AUTHORS

JANE O'REILLY:

Jane O'Reilly is the author of the Amazon bestselling space opera *Blue Shift* and the sequel *Deep Blue*. She likes Captain America and biscuits, and lives near London with her family.

You can find her on her Facebook page, on Twitter as @janeoreilly, or at her website www.janeoreilly.co.uk

KERRY BUCHANAN:

Kerry Buchanan hatched in the wilds of Yorkshire, but now nests in the wilds of County Down, not far from Ballynahinch.

She is a retired vet, stable hand, carer and dreamer who wrote her first novel in 2014. Since then, she has had short stories published both online and in print, and has occasionally been lucky enough to win prizes – and the competitions weren't even fixed. She writes science fiction, fantasy, and crime.

Kerry has been successful in several competitions, including a first place in Skypen (Blackstaff Press's competition for new writers, now defunct), and runner-up in Haynet and Lavender and White's equestrian-themed short-story competition, as well as winner of the 2015 Special Submissions Window for *Kraxon Magazine* with *The Survivor,* and third place in *Kraxon Magazine*'s short story of the year competition in 2014 with *Soul Ship.* Recent publications include *Matchgirls* in the *Bangor Literary Journal*, and she has a piece of flash fiction, *Only a Clockwork Heart*, accepted for an upcoming anthology, *The Bramley*, published by Armagh Flash Fiction.

You can find Kerry at kerrybuchanan.co.uk or in Twitter @Cavetraveller.

ROSIE OLIVER:

Rosie has been in love with science fiction ever since she discovered a whole bookcase of yellow-covered Gollancz science fiction books in Chesterfield library. She was very disappointed when she read the last of those novels. Her only option then was to write science fiction. Which is what she did after gaining two Masters degrees in mathematics, and a career in aeronautical turned systems engineering. To help her along the way, she gained an MA in Creative Writing from Bath Spa University, where her course novel was shortlisted for the Janklow and Nesbit prize as the most promising novel on the course.

Over twenty of her short stories have since been published in magazines, anthologies and as standalone e-books. Her story *Cyber Control* was voted the favourite short story in *Kraxon Magazine* in 2016. She published / edited the *SFerics 2017* anthology, from which one of the stories, *Angular Size*, by Geoff Nelder was shortlisted for the 2017 BSFA shorter fiction award. While writing her C.A.T. (a robo-cat) novel, she gained eight Honourable Mentions from the international Writers of the Future Contest, purr, purr, purr. She is currently concentrating on writing science fiction novels in different universes (yes, plural!).

You can find Rosie online at rosieoliver.wordpress.com.

JULIANA SPINK MILLS:

Juliana Spink Mills was born in England but grew up in Brazil. Now she lives in Connecticut and writes science fiction and fantasy. Sometimes her stories are dark. Sometimes there is kissing. Or stabbing — things could go either way, really. She is the author of *Heart Blade* and *Night Blade*, the first two books in the young adult Blade Hunt Chronicles urban fantasy series. Her short stories have appeared in anthologies and online publications. Besides writing, Juliana works as a Portuguese/English translator, and as a teen-library assistant.

Find out more about Juliana at jspinkmills.com, or by following her on Twitter @jspinkmills.

DAMARIS BROWNE:

Damaris Browne is a former solicitor whose ancestors include Spanish aristocrats, Somerset horse-dealers, numerous soldiers of various ranks from private to general, and one wife-murderer.

When not writing about SF alien judges and fantasy characters in historical settings (not yet both in the same novel), she spends her time reading, gardening, ignoring housework, and hanging around at SFFChronicles, where she's a moderator known as The Judge. She lives with her husband, cat, and a lot of books, on the edge of the New Forest National Park in England.

E.J. TETT:

E.J. Tett has been writing stories since primary school, some of which still survive in notebooks in her dad's attic, and wanted to be an author as soon as she realised it was a possible career choice and "pony" and "ninja" weren't viable options.

Her first short story, *Club Freak*, about an anonymous woman's determination to find her husband's killer, was published by Park Publications' *Debut* magazine in May 2009. Since then, she has gone on to write many short stories and poems for various small presses and has achieved an honourable mention in the 2011 Writers of the Future competition.

In 2014, writing as Emma Jane, she signed her first publishing contracts for not one, but two novels: *Otherworld*, formerly published by Torquere Press, and *Shuttered*, by Dreamspinner Press. She also has two novels published by NineStar Press, one a space opera and the other a contemporary romance.

Find E.J. online at ejtett.weebly.com and follow her on Twitter @emizzy.

SHELLIE HORST:

Yorkshire-born Shellie Horst is never far from a castle or a decent brew. As well as her freelance work, Shellie Horst writes science fiction and fantasy. Her fiction was first published in 2013. She is a regular contributor to SFFWorld, a popular science fiction and fantasy review site. She also organises HumberSFF, making the genre more accessible for fans across the Humber region.

Find out more about Shellie by visiting her website: www.millymollymo.com or following her on Twitter @millymollymo.

SUSAN BOULTON:

Like the song by The Police says, Susan Boulton was born in the '50s, and she had the unusual distinction of arriving into this world two hundred yards from where, thirty-seven years before, Tolkien spent time thinking about hobbits.

Susan has lived all her life in rural Staffordshire, and has a passion for the countryside, its history, myths and legends, all of which influence her work. Married with two grown daughters, Susan now puts her overactive imagination (once the bane of both her parents and teachers) to good use in her writing.

Susan is the author of *Hand of Glory* (Penmore Press) and *Oracle* (Tickety Boo Press). She has had short stories published in the following: *Flashspec* volumes one and two, published by EQ books; *Touched by Wonder*, published by Meadowhawk Press; *Ruthless People; Alien Skin; Golden Visions; The Dark Fiction Spotlight; Tales of the Sword*, published by Red Sky Press; *Malevolence – Tales From Beyond the Veil*, by Tickety Boo Press; and *Kraxon Magazine*.

You can find Susan at susanjboulton.co.uk or on Twitter @BoultonSusan.

JO ZEBEDEE:

Jo writes science fiction and fantasy, sometimes in her space opera world of Abendau, sometimes on the streets of her native Northern Ireland. She is supported by the Arts Council of Northern Ireland and, after the success of *Inish Carraig* where she destroyed Belfast in an alien invasion, is currently working on an all-new dystopic vision for her land.

As well as writing, Jo is the former chairperson of Women Aloud NI, an organisation dedicated to raising the profile of women writers in Northern Ireland, and founder of SFFNI, a group for speculative writers based in Northern Ireland. She's also active on the Irish convention scene as well as various book festivals and events throughout Ireland, and regularly delivers courses and workshops about writing.

She's had oodles of short stories published, has been listed in *The Guardian* as a "Top 10 Irish SF writer", has been an Amazon bestseller, and thinks that, for a supposed hobby, this writing lark is great craic altogether.

When not writing, Jo runs her own management consultancy and taxis teenagers to various places. She's considering cloning technology as a viable answer to her inbox concerns.

You can find Jo online at jozebedee.com or on Twitter @jozebwrites.

DISTAFF

45178185R00094

Printed in Poland
by Amazon Fulfillment
Poland Sp. z o.o., Wrocław